For Dad

KU-224-178

Priority Male

SUSAN KEARNEY

SILHOUETTE
INTRIGUE™

First published in Great Britain 1999
Silhouette Books, Eton House, 18-24 Paradise Road,
Richmond, Surrey TW9 1SR

© Susan Kearney 1998

ISBN 0 373 22478 8

46-9906

Printed and bound in Spain
by Litografia Rosés S.A., Barcelona

Chapter One

Jasmine Ross watched the only home she'd ever known turning to ashes.

Ashes.

It was all gone...her home...her computer business...her dreams.

She'd been lucky to escape alive.

Clutching her mother's music box, her only tie to her family, she gazed at the utter devastation. The humid air carried the reek of smoke and burning wood, and she ached to turn and run.

Instead, she watched the roof cave in, the hellish sparks shooting into the Florida sky.

Who had torched her home? And why? Rage poured into her empty heart, once filled with hope of her mother's returning to this house someday. A foolish hope now, amid her frustration and despair.

She had never known her father, not even his name, and her mother had disappeared when Jasmine was three. Now nothing remained for her mother to come back to. Gone was the home where Jasine had spent such happy days with her aunt. Gone was the security of operating her own computer school there. Gone was the hope her mother might one day return to this place—to her daughter.

Despite the arrival of fire trucks, hungry flames swallowed Jasmine's garage and car, inflaming the rage in her heart. She'd been lucky to get out with a pair of jeans, an old T-shirt and her backpack, which included her wallet. The house was insured and she could rebuild, but a new house would not hold the same memories.

Jasmine felt drained and weak as the walls caved in, and with them, the last of her hopes.

As she watched the firemen stow away their equipment, the postman, on his regular morning route, approached and, with a murmured word of sympathy, handed her a frayed and faded envelope. Return to Sender, stamped in conspicuous red, jumped out at her. Someone had initialed an attempted delivery date on the envelope. The return address matched the address of her house, now a smoking pile of rubble.

But *she* hadn't written to Mr. Talbot Moore in Dolphin Bay.

After the postman had given an explanation to Jasmine, a closer examination of the yellowed envelope revealed the handwriting wasn't hers, but resembled the neatly printed lettering of her mother's in Jasmine's baby album. After so many years of living without parents or family, except for Aunt Daisy, telling herself not to get worked up over a lost piece of mail did no good. Common sense told her this letter might shine some light on why, twenty-five years ago, Lily Ross had walked out of Jasmine's life without explanation.

She focused on the postmark, and shock burned her

tear-filled eyes. *May 8, 1973.* A few days before her mother had disappeared.

Although Jasmine knew nothing of her father, not even his name, she had vague recollections of her mother. Lily. When Jasmine listened to the soft tinkle of her mother's cherry-wood music box, these images were strongest. She was never certain if the memories were real or if she'd fantasized about her mother's soft, loving voice, her scent of wildflowers, the security of her good-night hug.

Jasmine had believed herself finally resigned to never knowing why her mother had left on an errand—and had disappeared. Her body had never been found, leaving her grieving sister Daisy to raise Jasmine, a child tormented by nightmares of abandonment. For years Jasmine had wondered if her mother had been murdered or abducted, while the awful possibility that perhaps Lily hadn't loved her enough to return and raise her haunted her dreams.

Swallowing the lump in her throat, Jasmine looked from the smoking ashes of her home back to the envelope, her eyes misty, her throat tight. Although she'd never heard of Talbot Moore in Dolphin Bay, that her mother had written him a letter kindled a wildfire of curiosity. With shaking fingers, she slit the envelope and removed the letter.

FROM THE MOMENT the taxi drove up the oak-shaded street and Jasmine Ross took in the gingerbread, three-story Victorian that was Moore House, the looming mansion seemed to suck all the oxygen from the air around her.

After matching the address on the faded envelope to the numbers on the red brick mailbox, she instructed the cab driver to pull into a wide circular driveway. Veiled by the green foliage of thick, moss-draped branches, the chocolate brown house suggested vastness, timelessness and a hint of forbidding secrecy.

In the twilight, she caught a glimpse here and there of a steep roof, a jutting balcony and a shingled turret. She studied the house, searching for traces of the owner's character, wondering about the man who lived there. But the immaculately maintained exterior couldn't talk, wouldn't reveal anything except an eerie sense of foreboding.

The covered porches along the front and sides held tight to their secrets. The image made her shiver and raised goose bumps on her skin.

She clutched her mother's music box for courage. Would she find her father here, as her mother's old letter had hinted? After hesitating a moment to inhale and exhale a deep breath to calm her nerves, Jasmine walked on unsteady legs up the front porch steps and pressed the doorbell. Would her father answer the door?

From inside the house, strident masculine voices deep in argument rose in volume. After waiting several long minutes, a wizened old woman in a maid's uniform opened the door. Her hair stood up in orange tufts like an orangutan's. "May I help you?"

"I'd like to speak with Mr. Talbot Moore."

The old woman frowned and started to close the door. "That's not possible."

Jasmine stuck her foot across the threshold. "It's urgent. I must speak with him."

At the sound of footsteps, the maid looked over her shoulder.

"Belle?" a man called out. "Is anything wrong?"

Was that her father speaking? But the voice sounded as if it belonged to a younger man.

"Someone's here, insistin' on speakin' to Mr. Talbot Moore," Belle said.

The maid left, and a dark-haired man appeared at the door and appraised Jasmine. A faint smile, no more than a slim curve, turned up the corners of his mouth, and black hair swung into his eyes. With a gesture of annoyance, he dragged a hand through his hair, shoving it back off his broad forehead. What had been dimples in youth had deepened to creases that could incite a woman's fantasies. But it was his steel gray eyes assessing her with intelligent yet cynical curiosity that had her thinking this man knew what he wanted and went after it.

"Yes?"

Her mouth dry as cotton, she moistened her lips. Had one of the male voices she'd heard belonged to her father? Were twenty-plus years of wondering about her father about to end? "Is this the Moore residence?"

"Yes," the man drawled lazily, his gaze lingering on the slight bruise on her brow and the cut on the back of her hand from her hasty escape of the fire. At another time she might have admired his rich baritone—soft, mellow and undeniably sexy. But she refused to let his voice distract her from her mission.

Hoping her trembling fingers didn't betray her nervousness, Jasmine held out her hand, stiffening her wrist to prevent a slight tremor. She met his gaze with a calm she didn't feel as he shook her hand. "I'm Jasmine Ross."

"Rand Sinclair." His words rippled through the

night air, warming her like caramel poured over ice cream. The evening breeze picked up the faint scent of sandalwood aftershave from his tanned skin. Radiating authority in his blue chambray shirt and khaki slacks, he looked every inch the owner of this house, a man who wasn't fazed easily.

Caught staring into his gray eyes, she looked away. She hadn't anticipated explaining her situation to anyone other than her father. Rand Sinclair was much too attractive, causing her thoughts to stray from her inquiry. Rand towered over her, but it wasn't just his height that she found both appealing and intimidating. His perceptive eyes could haunt a woman's dreams.

Under other circumstances, she'd have wished to know him better, but she didn't have time for dark and appealingly enigmatic men. "I was hoping to talk to Talbot Moore."

One dark brow arched with vivid interest. "About?"

"It's personal."

Clearly, he was accustomed to more straightforward answers. His shoulders stiffened slightly, and a thread of menace entered his baritone. "Talbot isn't…available."

"I can return later. Do you know when he might see me? It's important." She tucked the music box under her arm, hoping she'd masked her disappointment with a breezy tone.

His eyes bored into her. "Perhaps I can help you."

What was *his* relation to Talbot? she wondered, trying to ignore the slippery little fingers of fear gliding over her. Ever since the fire, she had been a mass of jangled nerves. She found herself fighting the instinct to confide in someone. After she'd almost been killed in the fire, she shouldn't trust anyone. But since this Rand Sinclair couldn't possibly know her connection to Talbot Moore, she shouldn't have anything to fear from him.

Still, all her instincts on alert, she sensed a trap. There was a stillness about the man that unnerved her, that wasn't just a by-product of the tension zinging between them. Sensing he wanted something from her, she shoved the speculative thought aside, determined not to stray from her objective. "Please. You must let me speak to him."

His mouth softened with compassion. "I'm sorry."

"I heard voices inside. Is he in the house?"

"You must be mistaken." His face displayed an uncanny awareness, as if he suspected she was here for ulterior reasons. His tone sharpened. "No one is home but Belle and me."

Jasmine had heard him speaking to *someone* male, and she hadn't expected outright denial of the other man's presence. She almost panicked, then squared her shoulders and firmed her lips. Rand's countenance was unreadable, and she wondered what he was thinking. What was it exactly about him that made her immediately curious, yet distrustful? His eyes conveyed a secretive gleam that intrigued her more than any welcoming smile.

Just from his substantial presence, she suspected he was one of those forceful men who take charge of any situation. She could easily imagine him starring in a James Bond movie, directing a boardroom of executives or driving a front-end loader.

She ignored his refusal, his treating her like a door-to-door salesperson, and made an effort to keep her tone matter-of-fact. "Please, let me talk to Mr. Moore."

Rand watched her like a hawk. "Talbot died three months ago."

Shock sent her reeling, pain had her fighting back tears. Her knees buckled. She would have fallen if Rand hadn't reached out to catch her in his strong arms.

He steadied her against his chest, practically dragged her into the dark hall and settled her on a bench. He sat beside her and kept a protective arm around her. "Hey, are you all right?"

Unable to speak past the lump in her throat, twisting the music box in her hands, she stared at the polished oak floor. After waiting a lifetime, she'd missed knowing her father by three months.

Three months.

Somehow she had to get hold of herself, phone for a taxi and leave. But between the shock of losing her home and business and this terrible news about her father, she surrendered to emotional overload and exhaustion.

Talbot Moore was dead. She struggled to accept that fact. Her mother's letter, implying that Talbot Moore was her father, had come too late. Now, just as fate had sent her to Moore House, fate had whisked her father away.

Shuddering, she closed her eyes and clenched her fists. It would feel so good to be held, to cradle her head against Rand's broad shoulder and melt into the strength of the arm he'd flung around her. But he was a stranger.

Even as she was grateful for Rand's support, she wondered why he had lied. She'd clearly heard him arguing with someone before she knocked on the door. Or had she? She was too overwrought to think straight.

When Rand remained silent, she risked another glance at his rugged face. His eyes weren't focused on her, which suited her fine. With the aura of power he emanated, she was sure he could be most intimidating—and just as sure she was in no shape to stand up to him. Yet at the same time, if she was honest, she found the coiled strength in him exciting. She needed a moment alone to collect her thoughts.

"Could I please have a glass of water?"

"Sure. I'll be right back." He stood and left without a backward glance, yet she sensed his suspicion of the stranger in his home.

No wonder she couldn't rid herself of almost frantic edginess. She had to cope, but for the first time in her life she had no one to help her. Her best friend was on a bike tour in Europe. Another friend had just married and moved to California. She wished she had parents or a husband, someone available to discuss and share her problems.

She reminded herself she was the same independent woman she'd been yesterday—before the letter, the fire and her knowledge of Talbot's death, before she'd practically collapsed in Rand Sinclair's arms. Suspicions racked her. Was it just coincidence that her mother had disappeared soon after her letter was first mailed, asking Talbot Moore for financial help in raising their child? Could her father have had a part in her mother's disappearance? The sinister question took root and blossomed. Perhaps Talbot Moore had refused to acknowledge Jasmine as his daughter. If her mother had been persistent, she might have enraged him to the point of violence. And now, was it just coincidence her mother's letter had turned up immediately after the fire? She'd never known her father's name until this morning. And with that name had come questions, suspicions. So why should news of his death hit her so hard that she wanted to cling to a stranger like a baby?

True, her life had changed drastically since this morning. But she couldn't crawl into bed and hide in dark misery. Hell, she didn't even have a bed—it had burned with the rest of her furniture.

Once she worked past the pain of loss, she would move on with her life. This wallowing in the past was unlike her. Welcoming a man's arms to comfort her was uncharacteristic. His heat made her too aware of him.

Nothing had prepared her for the devastation of the fire and the turmoil of her mother's old letter. Nothing had prepared her for a tall, dark stranger who seemed both compassionate and wary. Digging into her pocket for a tissue, she blew her nose.

She had once had a mother, owned her house, a car and a business. Now she had hoped to meet her father. No more. But she would adapt. She could rebuild her life, bury her past.

"Are you all right now?" Rand asked as he handed her the glass, his concerned voice breaking into her worries.

"I'll be fine." She sipped the water. A sudden thought burst through her misery. This man could be her half brother. "Are you Talbot's son?"

He sent her a peculiar look, as if surprised by her personal question. The hall lights flickered, throwing a dark shadow across his face.

Finally she got a response. "My dad and Talbot Moore were partners. After my folks died, Talbot raised me."

She almost spilled the water on the music box. Carefully she set down the glass.

Her father had raised him. She bit back a gasp as his revelation sliced razor sharp, and agonizing pain hit anew. She glanced down to hide the shock in her eyes. Her father had taken in someone else's child, while she'd had no father of her own.

When Rand was a child, had her father tucked him into bed at night, read him stories? Had her father held Rand on his lap after the boy skinned his knee? Taught him to use a computer? Catch fish? Play baseball? She shut down the unbearable train of thought.

Fighting back resentment, she tried to regroup. This wasn't going the way she'd planned.

She'd hoped to find Talbot Moore and clear up the mystery of her mother's disappearance. Instead, she'd confronted a painful truth. While she'd grown up without her parents, Rand Sinclair had been raised by her father.

She suddenly wanted to go home, climb into bed and sleep until the nightmare faded into oblivion.

Unfortunately, her situation was no nightmare but all too real, and her home was now in ashes—thanks to an arsonist. Her students wouldn't be waiting for her, not until she got the business back on its feet. And without her daily schedule to keep her mind on practical, humdrum matters, her thoughts kept skittering around the uncomfortable probability that someone wanted her dead. She covered her face with her hands, realizing she'd come to Dolphin Bay as much to escape whoever had burned down her house as she had to find out about her parents.

"What's wrong?" Rand's almost reluctant sympathy intruded on her worries.

She drew in another deep breath and raised her head. "Nothing."

He eyed her with a critical squint. "You don't look too good."

"I'm a little shaky. I'll be fine in a minute."

He regarded her suspiciously, and she guessed she hadn't hidden her pain very well. But she couldn't tell him the truth. And she couldn't escape her irrational jealousy.

She glanced down the somber hall to avoid his searching gaze. The house exuded a sense of substance, security and provoked a little awe. A rack for hats, coats and umbrellas stood by the door next to a grandfather clock. Two straight-backed chairs bracketed an oversize chest. Family pictures and etchings hung in a collection along one wall. Talbot Moore must surely be in one of them. Recalling that Talbot had been a father to Rand, but not to her, Jasmine couldn't bear to study the photographs.

To hide the reason for her earlier emotional response, she turned, faced Rand and grabbed the first explanation she could find for her odd behavior. "My house burned down this morning."

RAND CONCEALED HIS surprise behind his best poker face.

If Jasmine Ross was telling the truth, no wonder she was acting dazed and nervous. He had no reason to distrust her—except she had asked for Talbot as if believing him still alive. Plus, doubting everyone these days seemed prudent.

When Rand had first heard her speaking to Belle, he'd picked up a trace of panic in her tone. After he'd seen her wide eyes and the bruises on her face, he'd had only to lean forward to take in the scent of smoke. When she'd demanded to see Talbot, his suspicions skyrocketed. The fact that she felt so good in his arms couldn't deter him. He needed to learn why she'd come here asking about Talbot and to determine exactly what she knew.

More important—how much of the conversation in Talbot's library had she overheard?

He noted the bruise on her brow beneath her blond bangs and the skinned knee her hose couldn't hide. Her legs were dynamite—lean, muscular, sexy. But the fact that she hadn't bothered to hide the dark circles under her startling green eyes with makeup fascinated him. A good night's sleep might improve the pallor beneath her tanned face.

She was a puzzle he needed to solve. Escaping a fire would explain the assorted cuts on her hands. Still, she could have inflicted minor cuts and bruises to add authenticity to her story. But even after he'd informed her Talbot was dead, what would explain her constant glances toward Talbot's library, as if she expected him to walk over and join them any minute?

She was hiding something. And she didn't seem the type of person who would confide easily. But he couldn't let her walk away without answering his questions. Keeping Jasmine Ross at Moore House would provide a perfect opportunity to observe her, to discover what she knew. Judging from the haunted look in her green eyes and the paleness of her tawny, smooth skin, she had secrets of her own. When he'd told her no one else was home, she hadn't believed him, but had pressed her full lips together and swallowed hard. Did she know enough to pose a threat?

Had she come to pry information out of Rand? If so, she would be disappointed. His interest in the woman was unusual for him, and it had been too long since he'd crossed paths with anyone half as fascinating as Jasmine Ross, but he'd have no trouble keeping secrets from her. He held his liquor well. And he didn't talk in his sleep. Although, if Jasmine Ross was in his bed, he suspected he wouldn't get much rest.

What was he thinking?

She wasn't his type. He preferred experienced women who knew the score, rather than those with the vulnerability he sensed beneath this woman's outer shell. He steeled himself not to respond to her on a personal level.

What was she really doing here? And how much did she know about Talbot Moore?

Rand intended to check out her story. What personal business did she have with Talbot? Meanwhile, he'd keep his suspicions to himself and his tone purposely low, seductive. "I'm sorry to hear about the fire. Where did you live?"

"Seffner, a town just north of Brandon on the other side of Tampa."

She'd answered easily, without thinking. Either she was well rehearsed or telling the truth. But a local resident, even one on the other side of Tampa Bay, would have read the papers and heard the area news. She should have known about Talbot's death. Why had she pretended not to?

Her questions indicated that she could destroy his plans and everything he'd worked so hard to accomplish. For all his pragmatism, he usually relied on his instincts. Instinct told him to take her to bed. Common sense told him she was trouble and to stay away. If he was smart, he'd ignore her combination of vulnerability and strength that he found far too attractive.

He'd allowed the silence to last too long. Perhaps if he drew her into further conversation she'd confide in him or, at least, let something slip. "Were you hurt in the fire?"

She shook her head, and blond tendrils escaped her topknot and curled around her solemn face. "I never saw or heard the arsonist, but I smelled smoke and gasoline fumes from upstairs. I only had time to grab my mother's music box and my backpack before I got out."

"Arsonist? The fire was deliberate?"

Color slowly returned to her cheeks, though her bottom lip trembled. When she noted his perusal, she firmed her lips as if to hide her apprehension, and he enjoyed the laser gleam in her eyes. He considered taking her into his arms again and kissing the wariness from her lips, but she edged away. Smart woman. She must have sensed the danger inherent in being alone with him.

"Someone left a gas can in the yard. The fire was worst around the doors, blocking the exits. I barely escaped through a window."

So she suspected the arsonist hadn't just burned down the house, but had tried to kill her, too. Stunned, he forced a calm and sympathetic tone. "Sounds like you were lucky. And smart."

Her hands closed into fists. "I'm lucky to be here."

"I'm glad you are." From the way she kept peeking at the library door, she obviously didn't feel safe. Or could she be waiting for Talbot? That last possibility was crazy. And upsetting. "I suppose you've spoken to the police?"

"Idiots!" Disgust glimmered in her green eyes. "They think *I* set the fire to collect on my insurance."

Again she'd surprised him. This had to be the oddest conversation he'd ever had—but he couldn't pass up the opportunity to ask questions. "The police accused you?"

She took a long moment to curl a stray lock behind her ear. Although two nails of her long, slender fingers were broken, the others were clean and well shaped. Noticing his scrutiny, she clasped her hands protectively over the music box in her lap. "They say they're still investigating. But from their attitudes, I can guess what they're thinking."

Rand listened as he watched her mesmerizing fingers. Shoving aside the fantasy of her hands skimming his face, and puzzled by the police reaction, he rubbed his jaw.

Why would they suspect she had set her own house on fire? "Can you prove you're innocent?"

"Only if *I* catch the arsonist."

From her sarcasm, she obviously didn't think that likely. "Can you think of anyone who would want to harm you? A lover or husband, maybe?"

"My business keeps me too busy to have time for personal relationships," she answered without hesitation. Either she was innocent or lies came easily to her. "Now that my computers and business are gone...I should look for a job."

So she wasn't going to tell him *why* she'd come

looking for Talbot. Interesting. Keeping an eye on her had suddenly become a necessity. Fortunately, she'd just given him the excuse he needed to keep her at Moore House.

Chapter Two

Rand captured her gaze with a hypnotic stare. "Perhaps I can help."

Jasmine frowned. "I appreciate the thought, but I don't see what you can—"

"What kind of job are you looking for?"

Rand Sinclair's question thrilled her as much as the man himself puzzled her, but she kept her voice calm. "Secretarial, computer-related. Something temporary until the insurance company settles my claim and I can rebuild my house and business."

"I have a job for you."

His offer floored her. Her heart fluttered uncomfortably. She attempted to rein in her galloping pulse before he noticed the effect he was having. Damn her traitorous body for responding when her doubtful mind told her to resist him. Why was he being so helpful?

His intense eyes, direct and intrusive, made him appear dark, dangerous.

No, she definitely did not like the way he was looking at her. She edged toward the end of the bench, praying the maid might return.

When Jasmine didn't reply to his job offer, impatience rippled off him in waves. "Look, you'd be working for me here, at Moore House."

"What?" She couldn't believe her ears. Work at Moore House? Although just thinking about staying inside the old house gave her the creeps, she desperately needed a job. Her funds would only last so long.

More important, her number-one priority was to find out what had happened to her mother, which was the reason she'd sought to meet her father. She sensed answers here, smelled the mystery in the chilly, dank air, inhaled intrigue with every breath.

That Rand Sinclair had offered her a job so quickly only increased her suspicions. The man, no matter how darkly handsome, didn't appear to have any soft spots. He'd tendered the offer for his own reasons—and feeling sorry for her probably wasn't one of them. Clearly he had his own plan, and that made her more than uncomfortable. It made her wary. She had to stay alert, since someone apparently had intended to kill her by burning her house down around her.

From her mother's old letter, she now knew this house may have been one of the last places Lily had been before her disappearance. Jasmine ached to question Talbot's family, friends and neighbors about her mother and about why her father had never claimed her.

But no matter how much her past haunted her, no way would she place herself in danger to uncover twenty-five-year-old secrets. Better her curiosity went unsatisfied. She stood, carefully tucking the music box under her arm. "I couldn't work—"

"You could live at Moore House." His voice was deep, a little rough.

"No...thanks."

Rand didn't move from his seat on the bench. He watched her closely, a challenging glint in his shadowed eyes. She could use his help—if only she could be sure help was what he was really offering. What kind of game was he playing? She'd be a fool to participate when she didn't know the rules and was so obviously out of her league. And yet the only way to discover more about her father and what might have happened to her mother was to take the job.

The idea of living and working with Rand shot a tremor through her—though whether of excitement or fear she couldn't distinguish. He was a man of secrets, and she might be better off not learning what they were.

RAND WATCHED JASMINE'S charming face pinken, a flicker of anger mixing with wariness. She clutched the music box as a drowning woman would a life preserver. Had indignation at his suggestion caused the blood to rise to her cheeks and her eyes to darken like a wary doe's at a hunter's approach?

Flashing his most charming smile, he kept his tone sincere. "I'm setting up an office to work out of Moore House for a while, and I'll need a secretary here. Room and board are included, since I often work peculiar hours."

"Can I think over your offer?" she asked.

He nodded and walked her toward the front door, unwilling to let her slip away. She tensed, as if expecting him to try to stop her, but he simply gripped her elbow.

Beneath his fingers, her pulse beat faster than a hummingbird's wings. Why was she afraid? How much did she know? Her shrewd look suggested she discerned much more than she'd let on, and he suspected she had no intention of accepting his job offer. Damn. He'd have to change her mind.

He couldn't convince her without an explanation, but he couldn't tell her everything, either. If she knew the truth, she'd be ten times more frightened and screaming her lungs out for help.

Unfortunately, this time he couldn't blame his actions on his inability to resist a challenge or the tempting quiver in her lower lip. Nor was he simply satisfying his curiosity or adding a little excitement to his life. Keeping her at Moore House was a matter of life and death.

"Wait a minute." He released her elbow, and as she reached for the door, he blocked it with his body. "Look, why don't you have dinner, spend the night and consider my offer?"

She planted her feet and stared, skewering him with a look antagonistic enough to stop a Mack truck. "Why?"

Her eyes were too wide, the pupils dilated. She held her shoulders stiff as a soldier and appeared one step short of screaming for Belle. Sensing she was on the verge of bolting in panic, he debated how much to tell her. The last thing he wanted was for her to doubt his intentions. Better to calm her nerves. Releasing her arm had been a first step. He should have realized his size alone might frighten her, but he wasn't accustomed to having to ease women's fears. Usually they *wanted* to be with him.

But not Jasmine Ross. Her shrewd insight had warned her he wasn't on the level. Well, he'd just have to banish her suspicions.

"Why are you so intent on keeping me here?" Her words rushed together, revealing her fear.

"Because I want to make sure you're safe."

She tilted her head, eyeing him warily. "I don't understand."

"You said the fire at your house was deliberate. Talbot Moore died in a suspicious fire and the explosion that followed."

She gasped, staggered back a few steps and raised her knuckles to her mouth.

Was her intense reaction a sham? Fascinating. The woman had guts. And she was no dummy—which might make his task all the more interesting. Infinitely more difficult.

He retook her elbow and steered her away from the front door. "Why don't we talk in the study?"

She peered at him with vigilant green eyes, judging him with values he couldn't fathom.

He opened the study door.

In this room, where business and family accounts were settled, he and Talbot had often sat in comfortable chairs beside the fireplace after a game of billiards. This was one spot in Moore House where the drapes were always closed. While the others avoided the room, its dark solemnity had always soothed him. The dusky wood paneling and black walnut furniture suited the masculine atmosphere of the room.

Caution still lurked in Jasmine's expression, but her eyes were no longer rounded with fear. The pulse at her neck had returned to normal. She took in the business papers on the desk, the humidors that Talbot kept for guests, the decanters of port and brandy, and the fishing trophies.

As she stared at Talbot's collection of fossils and

old hunting equipment, she once again displayed her curiosity about the man, giving Rand the opportunity to study her. Without the dark circles beneath her eyes, she'd be attractive, although never gorgeous. Her eyes were set a bit too wide and her mouth a tad too full to qualify for model prettiness, but he found her latent vulnerability combined with her tough-minded refusal to confide in him appealing.

He pulled out a chair and offered her a seat. "Relax. Tell me why you came to see Talbot."

"I told you, it's personal."

"Look, I want to help."

She looked straight at him, bleak pain flickering behind her proud demeanor. "Why?"

"Why not?" he countered, unwilling to tell the truth. He rarely went out of his way to interfere in other people's lives. Didn't care to take on responsibilities that would involve his emotions. But meeting her had changed his plans. Now he had to decide what to do about her.

Her hands twisted in her lap. "Tell me about the fire that killed Talbot Moore."

"It's not exactly a pleasant story."

"Don't hold back on my account." Her tone was breezy, but he sensed the steel beneath.

He wouldn't tell her one fact more than she could have gleaned from old newspaper stories. "Talbot was inspecting a shopping center that our company, Sinclair and Moore Construction, was building. A fire started. Gas exploded and the entire building vaporized."

"Was it an accident?" She bored straight to the crux of the matter, exhibiting a keen intelligence he was beginning to appreciate.

"The police report said so."

"So why do you think *I'm* in danger?"

Watch yourself. She's sharp.

"I won't be sure until I know why you came to see Talbot. And I want to make sure you're safe."

Disbelief was written all over her frowning face. "So you invite me to stay in your home and offer me a job?"

He seated himself behind the desk to give himself time to think. "I want you to consider taking the job I offered." She blinked, an indication she'd noted his deliberate change of subject. Before she could say a word, he continued, "You see, I wasn't clear when I explained my offer of room and board to you."

"What do you mean?"

"I'm afraid I gave you the wrong idea. I wasn't making an improper advance. I don't live in Moore House alone. Besides me, Irene Moore, Talbot's widow, lives here. She's easy to live with—if you ignore her tendency to overreact to everything. In addition, Charles Wilcox, Irene's brother and our company attorney, lives here also."

She seemed to contemplate his offer, but he had trouble reading her tense expression. She replied without giving her feelings away. "Mrs. Moore might not like having a stranger under her roof."

"She won't mind."

"Aunt Daisy would never have taken in strangers."

Jasmine had spoken of her aunt in the past tense. She seemed so alone, but she might have parents, sisters or brothers, friends, people who depended on her, who would notice if she suddenly disappeared.

He needed to learn more before he took any irrevocable actions. "You live with your aunt?"

"Daisy passed away two years ago." She said the words tenderly, revealing how much she missed the woman. "Afterward, I converted part of the house to classrooms and opened a computer school."

"Irene won't mind an extra houseguest. Charles probably won't deign to notice you." Rand paused. Why was she so reluctant to stay at Moore House? "T.J., Art and Blain, Irene and Talbot's sons, aren't home enough to care if you move in."

From her stunned look, Rand doubted she heard the last half of his sentence. Before she could ask more questions, he pressed for an answer. "So do you want the job or not?"

JASMINE WISHED RAND wouldn't look at her with that bittersweet expression, which tugged at her in a way she didn't want to analyze. Had he guessed how much she needed to be here and offered the job as the excuse she needed to stay?

Rand probably didn't know that T.J., Art and Blain were her half brothers or how much she yearned to meet them. Shoving her misgivings to the back of her mind, she concentrated on the news she'd just learned.

She had family.

Would Talbot's sons look like her? More important, would they welcome a sister or want nothing to do with her?

Meeting long-lost brothers would be exciting, but she couldn't let down her guard. She must suspect everyone. Anyone could have torched her house—even one of her half brothers. But what would be his

motive, unless he had seen her mother's letter before
it was returned to Jasmine and now either knew or
guessed at Jasmine's relationship to Talbot? Had one
of Talbot's sons been driven to murder to protect
Irene from learning her husband had conceived a
child with another woman? Or for a motive more mer-
cenary?

She suddenly wondered if Talbot Moore, her obviously well-to-do father, had left a will. Surely if she
accepted Rand's job offer, she'd eventually learn the
answer. She might even find out what had happened
to her mother.

Rand waved his hand in front of her eyes. "Jasmine? You all right?"

"Sorry, I was thinking."

His eyes narrowed. "Is being my assistant that
tough a decision?"

She wondered why he was rushing her. Was he
simply impatient for an answer or did he have a more
sinister motive? Perhaps she was being overcautious.
Rand was gorgeous, wealthy and helpful. She had no
solid reason to suspect him of anything disreputable.
Besides needing a friend, she needed a job. And a
place to live. Accepting his employment offer would
solve her immediate problems. Once ensconced at
Moore House, she could learn about her father while
she secretly searched for clues to her mother's disappearance and for a reason why anyone there had
set her house on fire.

Still, she hesitated. "Why are you in such a
hurry?"

Rand glanced at his watch. "Charles should be
here soon, and I'd like our arrangement settled before
he arrives. I want you to tell him about the fire."

"Why?"

"As a favor to me, Charles will help you out. He has connections downtown. Although a fire in Seffner is out of this county, he can make unofficial inquiries, maybe hurry your insurance claim. He'll be home soon, before he heads into Tampa tonight for a Lightning game."

Relief flowed through her. She suddenly felt ridiculous for suspecting Rand Sinclair of harboring questionable intentions. He wanted her to talk to the family attorney. Who could be safer?

CHARLES WILCOX JOINED them a short time later, and Jasmine studied the attorney. Despite Charles' wrinkled face and gnarled hands, his energetic manner gave him the air of someone half his age. His eyes were brown, his chin sharp and his brows bushy, which she supposed made up for the lack of hair on his bald pate.

Rand leaned back in his chair. "Glad you got here. The lady was just about to leave."

"You must be losing your touch." Charles placed his briefcase on the desk and took a chair beside Jasmine. Rand quickly told him about her house burning down.

Jasmine spoke up. "Rand says you might be willing to help with my insurance claim."

"I'll do what I can. Police and fire investigations take time. You may have to be patient. So how did you get hooked up with this character?" Charles teased her, nodding toward Rand.

"He couldn't resist a lady in distress," Jasmine quipped, making light of how uneasy she had been here with Rand by herself.

Rand laughed, his white teeth flashing in his tanned face, and she caught her breath at how spectacular he looked. She was surprised some woman hadn't snapped him up ages ago. Something compelled her to respond to him, yet memory of the near-fatal fire raised her resistance.

Rand absently fingered an onyx chess piece, and she couldn't stop herself from admiring his hands smoothing the delicate rook. He had strong wrists with a dusting of dark hair on muscular forearms, long fingers with clean, clipped nails and calluses on his palms and fingertips.

Porch light peeked through a crack in the drawn drapes and illuminated Rand's dark eyes. He toyed with the rook, seemingly lost in thought, but not for one moment did she think he'd forgotten her.

Charles loosened his tie. "What else do I need to know about the fire?"

"The gasoline was worst around the doors," she told him.

"As if someone was trying to block her escape," Rand added.

She twisted her hands in her lap. "The fire investigators said the gas can they found on the lawn had been wiped clean of prints."

Charles's eyes narrowed. "Can you think of anyone who would want to harm you?"

Although she'd been reluctant to confide in Rand, his bringing in the family attorney *had* reassured her. Rand seemed sincere in his effort to help her. Deciding there was no longer any point in hiding her past, she reached into her backpack and withdrew her mother's letter to Talbot. "I think this letter started my problems."

Rand leaned forward for a better look at the envelope. When he spotted Talbot's name and address, his eyes widened. "What's inside?"

"A letter my mother wrote over twenty-five years ago. By the postman's scribble on the envelope, you can see a delivery attempt was made to Moore House last week."

Rand stared at the handwritten note, then at the postmark, and he raised his brows. "I've heard of snail mail, but twenty-five years to cross Tampa Bay is ridiculous."

"How did this happen?" Charles patted her shoulder soothingly as if he understood how many shocks she'd withstood this day.

"The postman said they're renovating the Dolphin Bay post office. When workers moved furniture in a storage room last week, a carpenter found an old sack of undelivered mail."

Jasmine had explained the easy part of her story first. But now she chose her words carefully and took a deep, bracing breath before continuing. "Mr. Moore's death explains why the letter came back marked Return to Sender. I live at the return address, so the letter was returned to me."

"Actually, the letter should have gone to the executor of Talbot's estate." Charles's brown eyes warmed with compassion. "That must have been strange. Imagine the odds of getting a letter back after all these years. What did your mother say about the letter?"

"Lily walked out of the house to go shopping when I was three years old, shortly after this letter was mailed. She never returned."

Charles sucked in his breath. "Was she ever located?"

"She was never heard from again." Jasmine spoke calmly, hiding the never-ending pain that telling the story caused.

"I'm sorry, but I have to ask." Rand gave her a sympathetic look. "Was her body found?"

"No," she said.

Charles winced at her words, and Rand focused on the letter, trying to make out the writing. "What does the letter say?"

"In many places, the words are smeared, so the writing is illegible. However, parts are quite clear." Jasmine pushed a stray tendril of hair from her face. "My mother asks Talbot Moore for financial help to support their child."

Charles blinked. His mouth gaped open and he stared at her. "Oh, my. Are you sure?"

Rand let out a long, low whistle of surprise, but his expression gave away nothing. "You're Talbot Moore's daughter?"

She nodded. "I never knew my father's name until I received this returned envelope today."

Charles peered at the letter and frowned as if he couldn't quite believe her. "What's the date on the postmark?"

"May 8, 1973," Jasmine said.

At the direction Charles's questions were taking, Rand grimaced, clear disapproval on his face. "A year before Irene married Talbot."

"You can be sure my sister will be glad to learn her husband hadn't been unfaithful." Charles spoke slowly, working out the implications.

While the men discussed Irene's feelings, Jasmine's chest tightened with disappointment and her thoughts veered from their conversation. When she was born, her father had been single. Had he chosen not to marry her mother? Chosen not to claim his child?

Despite the hollow ache caused by unanswered questions, she told them about her childhood. "My Aunt Daisy raised me, and then I took care of her until she passed away two years ago. My mother had told Aunt Daisy that my father died before I was born and refused to mention his name." Jasmine couldn't prevent bitterness from creeping into her tone. "I can't help but wonder what else my mother lied about. Maybe I don't want to know the truth."

Rand shook his head. "Of course you do. That's why you came to Moore House. But unfortunately, we don't have any answers. Your news surprised us, too."

Had it? Jasmine sensed Rand was hiding something, but she didn't know him well enough to be sure. Perhaps she was just upset.

"Maybe Irene knows what happened, but she's never mentioned any of this to me," Charles said. "Remember, your mother may have lied about your father to protect her reputation. Claiming to be an unwed mother with a dead lover was more acceptable to most folks back then compared to admitting they simply hadn't married."

Rand suddenly walked around the desk and took her hand. He squeezed lightly. Although his eyes were still unreadable, his hands were warm and offered comfort. "It's easier to tell a child her father is dead than to explain—"

"That Talbot didn't want me," Jasmine said with

a catch in her voice, wondering if Rand could feel her fingers trembling. The scent of sandalwood was mixed with the clean aroma of soap, and again, she wanted to bury her face against his shoulder, take comfort in his warmth.

What was wrong with her? Because she'd grown up without parents, she'd been an object of pity as a child. But hadn't she learned to stand on her own a long time ago? Just as she no longer needed a mother's advice or a father's approval, she didn't require a man's arms around her now to feel good about herself.

All her life she'd pretended she was like other kids who had big families. But she'd only had Aunt Daisy. Jasmine had worked hard to make up for the lack of parents, grandparents, sisters, brothers and cousins by throwing herself into her schoolwork.

After she'd grown to adulthood, she'd taken care of Aunt Daisy and built her business. She'd understood that being alone hadn't been her fault. She'd grown strong and self-reliant. Yet, the painful childhood memories had returned to haunt her. "Now I'll never know why my father didn't acknowledge me."

"Times were different then," Charles said kindly. "Maybe Talbot couldn't face the scandal."

Jasmine pulled herself together. "Better his child should grow up without a father?"

"Those actions don't sound like the man I knew," Rand said. "Talbot always lived up to his responsibilities. More likely your father was never told about you. And, after all, he never received that letter."

"I suppose."

"All right," Charles said. "Let me get this straight. Someone burned your house down, then you received this letter. There might be a connection between two such odd events, or they simply could be coincidence. Is there anything else you haven't told me?''

At Charles's assessment, a chill shimmied down her spine. The postman's scribble of an attempted delivery date and his initials indicated someone at Moore House had returned the letter in just the past few days. Had someone in this house *known* Jasmine was Talbot's daughter?

A day or two after the letter had been returned from Moore House, someone had burned down her home and tried to kill her. Had the person who'd seen her letter at Moore House started the fire? Had the men put together the fact that she suspected someone at Moore House of arson? If so, they certainly weren't admitting it.

Gathering her spinning thoughts, she answered Charles's question. ''I don't know what is important and what isn't. I'm not sure whom I can trust.''

Charles patted her shoulder again. ''You haven't given me much to go on. But let me do some checking. I'll have one of my contacts review the arson files. Meanwhile, I'll pressure the insurance company to pay your claim.''

AFTER CHARLES LEFT, Jasmine told Rand she would accept his job offer. She didn't tell him she'd stay only a few days, long enough to meet her half brothers. Vowing to keep her eyes and ears open, she refused to trust anyone, including the handsome man beside her.

Shivering in the gloomy study, she wondered if she'd ever feel warm and safe again.

''Cold?'' Rand asked. Perceptive, he noted her

every move, and she couldn't forget the warm comfort of his hands on hers, or the hard look in his eyes while Charles questioned her.

"I'm fine." She leaned back and smoothed the cherry wood on her mother's music box, thankful she'd saved her most precious possession from the fire. She had told Rand so much about herself, but she knew hardly anything about him. "So, tell me how a busy executive can work at home?"

He grinned, a smooth, delightful smile that lit up his face and made her breath catch. "I have employees I trust. And I delegate. Life's too short to spend all of it in an office, don't you think?"

"I've never had that luxury." She'd thought he might take the opportunity she'd given him to boast about his success. The few men she'd dated always talked about themselves. But Rand was different.

"That's because you started your computer school from scratch?" he guessed.

She nodded.

"My father and Talbot had the company well established before I came along and expanded on their solid customer base and well-earned reputation."

"What was my f-father like?" she asked, stumbling a bit over the word.

"Talbot?" Rand began to pace. She could almost hear the gears grinding in his mind while he recalled and filtered memories to describe her father.

"He was married to the job, a workaholic, conservative, honest, loyal and shrewd. He wasn't happy unless he was busy, physically and mentally. He enjoyed a good game of chess and loved dogs, although Irene wouldn't allow one in the house."

"Were he and Irene happy?"

"Talbot wasn't home much and rarely spoke about his private feelings."

"But did he have a happy marriage?"

"Irene worshiped your father." Rand spoke in a voice she found hard to read. "She ran the household around his schedule, instructed the cook to prepare the meat-and-potato dishes he preferred. But was he happy?" Rand shrugged. "How can someone else really know? Talbot was often quiet, thoughtful. When I was a kid, I always knew he was on my side. Even when I'd done something wrong, I could go to him."

How different would her life have been if Talbot had been there for her—especially after her mother disappeared? How many times as a child had she cried herself to sleep after wrapping herself in her mother's nightgown, wishing she had parents like the other kids? As a child, she'd always longed for a large family, dreamed of holiday gatherings and of enjoying a closeness she would never have.

Since Aunt Daisy's death, she had been alone. As painful as it was to hear Rand speak about her father, she was eager to hear more. After not knowing about Talbot for so many years, she couldn't stop asking questions.

When Rand halted in front of her, she tensed, instinctively lowering her voice. "Did Talbot ever talk about the time before he was married?"

Rand shook his head. "Come to think of it, he never did."

Well, that line of questioning had come to an abrupt dead end. Although Irene Moore might know something about the time Talbot had spent with her mother, Jasmine would have to approach the topic carefully. Rand and Charles had already hinted Irene wouldn't be happy to learn of Jasmine's existence.

She wondered again who at Moore House had returned her mother's letter. The envelope had been delivered here, but then returned. Could someone have opened the letter, learned of Jasmine's existence and then set her house on fire? Had Irene Moore hated her so much that, sight unseen, she'd attempted to kill her? If so, why return the letter at all?

Jasmine's suspicions of Irene seemed far-fetched. Although women were rarely killers, it did happen, yet most of the violent offenders in prison were men. And she doubted a woman who had lived as a society matron would suddenly turn into a murderer.

Murderer or not, Irene Moore wasn't going to be happy with Jasmine under her roof. It remained to be seen whether her half brothers would welcome her. What had she gotten herself into?

JASMINE TOSSED UNDER the covers, unable to sleep in the spacious room Rand had given her. Although immaculate, the room held the faint odor of mold, and its tired walls of dark paneling added to the gloomy atmosphere. Moonlight shone through the windowpanes, casting menacing shadows, enclosing her and the four-poster bed and canopy in a cocoon of binding silver threads. But it was the creaks and groans of the old, dreary house with its secrets of the past that had Jasmine thankful for the secure lock on her door.

From the moment her taxi had driven up the oak-shaded drive to the three-story Victorian that was Moore House, she had felt her destiny calling, but that destiny remained shrouded.

She couldn't force these dark rooms to give up secrets any easier than she could the tall stranger sleeping now in the room next door—but whether or not Rand's presence was a plus or minus, she wasn't sure. The thought made her shiver and raised goose bumps on her skin, despite the sweatshirt that Rand had lent her to sleep in. She pulled the comforter closer to her chin, grateful for its warmth.

Although Rand said that her three half brothers, Irene and Charles lived here, Jasmine had seen no one but the attorney and Belle, who'd gaped at Jasmine but had been pleased to serve them tonight, even when she'd expected everyone to be gone.

Rand had led Jasmine to believe the two of them wouldn't be alone in this gloomy mansion, assuring her Irene would be back from a charity function late, as would Charles from his hockey game, and that her brothers usually came home in the evening. But it was half-past two and she hadn't yet heard a car drive into the garage.

Had Rand lied about the others living here? Her initial doubts about him had lessened after he'd introduced her to Charles. She had to caution herself that Rand and Charles were business associates, and a small-town attorney could be unprincipled. A law degree no longer meant absolute honesty.

The wind blew, whistling around the corners of the house, creating a draft in the chimney of the bedroom's empty fireplace. Perhaps the flue wasn't closed. Jasmine burrowed deeper under the covers, wishing she was at home and Aunt Daisy was downstairs, coming up to tuck her in for the night.

She hadn't felt safe, not even when Rand had comforted her so gently. Right now, amid the strange shadows along the walls, she could use a little security. Reaching for her mother's music box, she wound the key, hoping the familiar music would soothe her.

The floor squeaked in the room next door and her heart thudded. A few minutes later, water whooshed through pipes and she realized Rand might just now be going to bed and not already asleep as she'd assumed.

Slowly sheer exhaustion overtook her. Her body heat, trapped by the quilts, warmed the feather mattress. Her muscles slowly relaxed, and she sank into a deep sleep, fraught with nightmares.

Someone turned the knob of her bedroom door. It swung wide, silently. Footsteps shuffled across the hardwood floor.

Terrified, Jasmine didn't move. Holding her breath, she peeked out between barely opened eyelids.

A black, shapeless shadow loomed at the foot of her four-poster bed. Dark, menacing, the silhouette advanced. She heard raspy breathing. Her throat closed so tight, she couldn't scream. Heart pounding, she pulled the covers over her head.

Chapter Three

Jasmine, frightened and confused, no sooner pulled the covers over her head than she yanked them down again and surged upright. She didn't know what she would do if a killer stood at the foot of her bed. But hiding wouldn't save her.

Squinting into the darkness, she spied only nebulous tones of black and blacker. No spooky silhouette hovered over her bed. The room was empty.

Had she wakened from a nightmare and imagined the looming shape? Flipping on a dim lamp that cast a murky green glow into the dark corners of the room, she hefted a paperweight from a bedside nightstand as a weapon and searched the room with a cursory glance. The mirror hanging over the dower chest reflected back her wide eyes in a too-pale face, but no one loomed over her, not even a hint of a ghost. She appeared to be the sole occupant of the antique-filled room.

Padding on chilled bare feet to the door, she found it shut tight, locked as she had left it. Feeling foolish, she retreated to her bed, brushed aside the floral chintz hangings and knelt on hands and knees to check under the four-poster. Satisfied no one was hiding there, she stood and searched the closet, then carefully replaced the paperweight beside her mother's music box and plopped onto the mattress. Although relieved she was alone, she remained reluctant to turn off the light.

Had she dreamed the footsteps, the raspy breathing, the dark silhouette? It had seemed so real. Yet, in these strange surroundings, an odd nightmare or two wouldn't be unusual.

As her pounding heart slowed, she considered her options. She could call the police, which seemed an overreaction. She could leave Moore House in the morning. Or she could stay and chalk up the episode to a nightmare.

The nightmare option was the most practical solution.

As far as Jasmine knew, no one besides Rand was aware she was in the room. Had he told someone? Tomorrow she'd ask him if anyone else had a key to her door. Perhaps one of her brothers had come by to check on her. But she couldn't help but dwell on the more sinister implications of an uninvited late-night visitor. If clues to her mother's fate existed at Moore House, would someone try to harm her or frighten her away?

A thorough search of her room the next morning revealed nothing unusual. No one had touched her few possessions. As she showered, dressed and went in search of Rand, her stomach fluttered in nervous anticipation of meeting her half brothers and her father's widow.

After heading downstairs, Jasmine entered the dining room, where elegant antiques and art decorated every inch of space. Brilliant sunlight, a jewel-toned

Tiffany window and a venetian chandelier cast cheerful prisms of light across the business section of the *St. Petersburg Times* and the young man reading the business section at the dining table.

He looked up with a flash of irritation, smoothly hid his annoyance and favored her with a gracious expression as he rose to his feet. At the shape of his familiar green eyes, her heart beat crazily. She recognized those eyes, the exact shade as her own. His dark brown hair was so neat that she longed to muss it, and his arrogant eyebrows rose upward and upward. She assumed he was one of her brothers.

She cleared her throat and offered to shake hands. "Good morning. I'm Jasmine Ross."

"T.J. Moore."

T.J.'s tone was clipped, curt, his eyes watchful. He shook her hand, the polite gesture of a Southern gentleman greeting a houseguest or a stranger, but he didn't draw her into a hug, the welcome she'd hoped for. Perhaps he didn't yet know they were related.

His palm was cool and damp. Possibly, he'd just set down the glass of orange juice next to his unfinished breakfast. Or was he nervous? Did he somehow know her identity and was warily waiting to see if she'd recognize him as the person who'd sneaked into her room last night?

At close range, T.J.'s agitation was more noticeable. A muscle ticked in his jaw and his eyes, so like her own, darted away, his gaze slipping past the vicinity of her right ear as if he couldn't bear to look at her. Yet, when he smiled, a quirky, wrenching smile that revealed straight white teeth and boyish charm, she decided he was simply nervous about meeting a stranger.

His eyes shifted, almost meeting her gaze. "Rand told us who you are."

"He did?"

Was Rand already awake? She hadn't heard a sound coming from his room, although she supposed he could have risen while the running water of her shower muffled his footsteps.

T.J. nodded, his expression watchful. "Except for Blain, who didn't come home last night, the entire family got together and Rand told us about you."

How was that possible? She hadn't heard one car pull in the drive. That Rand had already told the Moore family about her made her uneasy. Why hadn't she been included in the discussion? It appeared as if they'd deliberately considered what to do about her while she hadn't been around to listen.

She couldn't think why they'd excluded her from that conversation. Perhaps she should have heeded her first instinct about danger here and fled.

Stop jumping to conclusions.

For all she knew, no one had been at the foot of her bed last night. In the bright, cheerful light of the breakfast room, with the delicious aroma of hot bread and strawberry jam making her mouth water, her nighttime worries seemed foolish. The room conveyed feelings of security and solidarity. Walls covered with rich paper, wood paneling and ornate wood moldings framed substantial pieces of furniture. Jasmine allowed the pleasant room to calm her churning suspicions.

And she *was* grateful to Rand that she needn't go through the whole story again with each family member. "I didn't hear a thing."

T.J. shrugged. "It's a big house, and Rand put you

in the guest room away from the back drive.'' He gestured toward the sideboard holding steaming food in covered serving dishes of blue-and-white porcelain, a pitcher of orange juice, a plate of toast and a pot of coffee. "Help yourself to breakfast.''

At his admission that he knew in which room she'd slept, Jasmine was too nervous to think about food. Did everyone normally use the back driveway? There was so much about this family she didn't know, little things she needed to learn, like who had a key to her room and who had returned her mother's letter. Hiding her spinning thoughts, she helped herself to a cup of coffee and took a chair opposite T.J.

Ignoring his newspaper, T.J. stiffened his lips. "Mom's been grieving since Dad died. Don't do anything further to upset her.''

"We haven't even met,'' she protested, sensing an inherent polite streak in T.J. along with a ruthless intensity that good manners couldn't quite hide. There was much more he wasn't saying.

"I'm not blaming you,'' he said in a respectful tone. "But your timing could have been better.''

"Excuse me?''

His fingers closed into a fist. "This is a very awkward time for you to show up.''

She peered at him over the rim of her raised coffee cup. "Any time would have been awkward.''

"Maybe.'' A stern forthrightness entered his tone. "Dad passed away only a few months ago, and Mother hasn't yet adjusted to life without him. Now, not only must she deal with the loss of her husband and his past indiscretions, but with you, too. Your coming here now is not the best of ideas.''

His explanation was vague enough to make her

edgy, specific enough to make her wary. Dealing with computer spreadsheets was so much easier than understanding the complexities of people. Computers were logical. People rarely said exactly what they meant.

Was there a hostile edge to T.J.'s courteous request? She didn't know him well enough to read between the lines of his outwardly reasonable concerns. And while his protectiveness toward his mother was admirable, Jasmine didn't care for the way he deftly avoided a direct answer to her questions.

Swallowing the coffee, which spread like courage down her throat, she nailed T.J. with a direct look. "What are you really saying?"

When his eyes, dark and fervent, swept her with a sincerely wounded air, she suspected he was trying to manipulate her. "If you leave Moore House until—"

"Jasmine's not going anywhere." Rand's words, rich and smooth as the finest wine, were polite but chilly. He entered the room, looking more handsome than any boss should. Admiring his tall frame and the impeccable fit of his clothes, she ignored the shiver of warmth that slid into her belly as she watched him walk in. Irritation at T.J.'s suggestion hardened the planes of Rand's face. Tight lines narrowed his eyes while his mouth twisted in a wry parody of a smile.

At Rand's declaration, she didn't know whether to feel thankful for his defending her right to be at Moore House or annoyed that he'd interrupted T.J. before she'd discerned his real motivation for asking her to leave.

And what of Rand's motives? His strong reaction to T.J.'s attempt to be rid of her indicated that her staying meant more to him than he'd let on. She fought to hide her roiling emotions. She couldn't show that she suspected Rand of hiding some ulterior reason for insisting she stay.

"Really?" A nerve twitched in T.J.'s lip. Apparently he wanted to say a great deal more.

Jasmine detected distrust between the two men. Tension mounted while Rand helped himself to scrambled eggs, crisp bacon and a strawberry muffin.

Orange tufts of hair tucked under a turban, Belle bustled into the room with a large glass of ice, poured Rand what looked like fresh-squeezed grapefruit juice into his glass and left. Her timing was curious. Had she been anxious to hear the conversation or was she just doing her job?

Rand snapped open a napkin, and Jasmine almost jumped at the sound. "Jasmine will be working as my personal assistant at the house."

T.J. shook his head. "You have a perfectly good secretary at work. Besides, there's no need to set up an office at Moore House and disturb Mother."

The conversation had taken an unexpected turn. As Jasmine observed these two powerful men who had grown up together, she saw more than a clash of eyes. The room charged with the clash of wills. With his need to protect Irene, T.J. had challenged Rand, practically accusing him of disturbing his mother. While on the surface all was gentlemanly, Jasmine sensed an undercurrent of deep-rooted animosity between the two men.

Her impulse to flee Moore House was suddenly stronger than ever as she questioned whether she could rely on Rand to help her. Perhaps she worried for no reason. Was T.J. simply protective of his mother? Or did *he* have an ulterior reason for wanting her away from Moore House?

She couldn't ignore the possibility that Talbot had confided in his eldest son about Jasmine's mother before he'd died. Did T.J. fear that if Jasmine remained at Moore House, she might discover what had happened to her mother? And if Jasmine *was* in danger, could Rand protect her?

RAND SET UP the office in an extra room on the third floor. While he removed files from boxes and placed them into a desk drawer, Jasmine's fingers danced over the keyboard as she installed software onto the new computer system. She chewed her full bottom lip in concentration, her gaze glued to the monitor, giving him an opportunity to observe her.

At ease with her work, she looked young, vulnerable and determined to prove she could do the job in front of her. While he couldn't complain about her efficient and professional work habits, he needed to encourage her to open up.

He had his work cut out for him if he intended to gain her trust. She was friendly enough, but kept a distance as if she had a great deal to hide. While his assessment might be completely inaccurate, his instinctive doubts continued. Reminding himself he had no real evidence against her, he watched her closely.

With her eyes focused on the screen, her face was pale, her shoulders set. Damn T.J. for upsetting her. Rand had hoped she'd be more amenable to answering his questions this morning, perhaps relax her guard and reveal what she was up to. But ever since T.J.'s outburst at breakfast, she'd been unusually quiet.

After placing the last of the files in his desk, he peered over her shoulder. "T.J. will come around. Talbot's death brought out his protective instincts and he's worried about Irene."

"Do the other's also feel I'm a threat?" She didn't miss a beat on the keyboard, but the quaver in her voice gave away her raw feelings.

Deliberately distracting her, Rand touched the scrape on her wrist. She immediately stopped typing and glanced up, curiosity mixed with sadness in her eyes. When she didn't jerk away, he skimmed the pad of his thumb over her pulse. Her skin was soft and silky, the scrape a stark reminder that she'd barely escaped the fire.

Feigning a casualness he didn't feel, he laced his fingers in hers and gently led the conversation toward the danger surrounding them. "Blain, the youngest son, didn't come home last night, so he doesn't know about you yet. But the rest of us feel trouble may follow you here."

Her eyes widened with an unfathomable look, but her shoulders stiffened, her gaze locking determinedly with his. "Do *you* want me to leave?"

At the vulnerability in her eyes, Rand's taut control almost snapped. He'd been watching her with a mixture of conflicting emotions. Desire, admiration, regret—anger at himself for the necessity of his lies, tempered by the fact he couldn't trust her enough to tell her the truth. "No one wants you to leave—not even Irene."

"But T.J. said—"

"You can't believe everything T.J. says. He'd say anything to protect his mother."

Her head shot up and she shivered as if suddenly

chilled, but he was sure her trembling had little to do with the cool air. It took every ounce of his control not to take her into his arms. Obviously, he'd frightened her, hopefully enough to keep her wary, but not enough to make her leave.

He squeezed her hand lightly. "T.J.'s simply afraid Irene can't endure a scandal."

As if sensing the battle he fought, Jasmine snatched back her hand and rolled her eyes at the ceiling. "It's not as if I've taken out a full-page ad in the newspaper announcing that I'm Talbot Moore's daughter."

"True." Fighting the approval rippling through him at her courage, he eased his hip onto the corner of her desk. "But Dolphin Bay is a tight-knit community. Many residents have lived here for decades. In Irene's social circles, the news of Talbot's indiscretion will travel faster than a hot stock market tip."

"I take it Talbot was a faithful husband?" She said the words slowly, as if trying to understand the complicated man who'd been her father. Rand had to keep reminding himself of her point of view. Talbot, the upstanding pillar of the community he'd respected, who had taken in an orphaned boy, had never met his daughter.

Rand also had to remember she was Talbot's daughter. He owed it to the man who had given him a home to keep his hands off her. Only he never expected it to be so difficult. He couldn't deny the tension between them. Moore House was like a battlefield, every word guarded, every movement gauged for weakness, every strength honed. His actions had to be limited to the part he played. He couldn't help wishing that those curious eyes layered with wariness would look at him differently. He longed to kiss the skepticism off her lips, and see if she tasted as delicious as she looked.

Resisting the impulse, he folded his arms over his chest and told her what he could. "Talbot was a rock. We all counted on him to do the right thing. Whether in his personal life or in business, he took the high road. Even his competitors had only good things to say about him."

Her lips drew into a pretty frown. "Someone may have wanted him dead."

Just when he'd thought he was mistaken, that she had to be innocent, she threw another zinger. What did she know that made her so suspicious? She couldn't be oblivious, not when she so skillfully hinted at what not even the police suspected. She was a good actress—turning those incredible eyes toward him, tightening her bottom lip to prevent a quiver. He couldn't let her wide-eyed, guileless look prevent him from seeking answers. He hated to play hardball, but if she wanted in the game, she had to expect to get dirty.

His matter-of-fact tone hid his inflamed curiosity. "You didn't know Talbot. Why do you think someone wanted to kill him?"

She arched a delicate eyebrow. "*You* told me he died in a suspicious fire."

Replaying his brief explanation to her yesterday, he realized again she was sharp. Clever of her to throw his own words back at him.

"So what happened?" she prodded. "What was suspicious about the fire?"

For once Rand didn't mind postponing work. Listening to her soft questions and learning how her mind worked fascinated him. He'd been mired in suspicions so long he couldn't make up his mind about her. How could her guiltless gaze say one thing while her perceptive questions indicated something else entirely?

Jasmine Ross confused him. She didn't act like a greedy woman after her father's inheritance. But why else would she be here?

He had to handle things between them carefully. Although he wanted to trust her, he didn't dare. She measured him, her expression relaxed, but she didn't seem entirely candid. If only he could tell her the truth about Talbot. But he couldn't.

Danger surrounded her as if she stood in the eye of a hurricane. The tiniest misstep could suck both of them into a maelstrom, dash her into an early grave.

"Three months ago, Talbot was at a construction site, inspecting the electrical wiring when the fire broke out."

"You'd mentioned an explosion."

"The fire heated an acetylene tank used by welders. The resulting blast incinerated the building."

She shook her head, and a lock of hair fell in her eyes. Restlessly, she shoved it away. "I don't understand. What was suspicious?"

"There was no reason for a welder to have been on the job. Our company hadn't hired a welder. Neither had our subcontractors."

Her brows drew together. "You think someone murdered my father?"

"Many people knew he'd scheduled a site inspection." Rand debated how much more to tell her. "But there were other incidents."

"Incidents?"

"Talbot had two other close calls the month before

he died. His fishing boat caught fire, but he escaped in the dingy.''

Her eyes, more uncertain than he'd ever seen them, searched every inch of his face. ''Caught fire?''

Rand nodded, appreciating how she cut to the important facts. ''Talbot also owned a cattle ranch in Brooksville. One night while he was sleeping there, the cabin burned down.''

''Another fire?'' Her face paled, as if she'd acknowledged the possibility that the same person who'd murdered Talbot might also be after her.

Why wasn't she demanding police protection? Was it because she wasn't in any danger? All Rand's earlier wariness rushed back. He had only her word that she hadn't known Talbot was her father until she'd received the letter.

Could she have set her own home on fire to cover her tracks and lessen Rand's suspicions about her motives? As he gazed at her trembling lower lip, he couldn't believe her capable of such deviousness. But looks could be deceiving, and she had much to gain from Talbot's death. Perhaps a lifetime of resentment against her father had driven her to act irrationally.

Yet if she hadn't known Talbot was her father until the old letter had been returned to her, she couldn't have been behind the construction-site explosion. A hard knot balled in his stomach. And if she wasn't the arsonist, then someone was after her, too.

A knocking on the door caused Jasmine to jump.

Irene opened the office door while patting her head to ensure every hair was in place. ''Excuse me, I wanted to meet our guest and make sure her room is comfortable.''

Without waiting for an invitation, Irene entered the

room and embraced Jasmine, engulfing her in magnolia-scented perfume. "Are you all right dear? I heard there was a dreadful fire...."

Every once in a while, Rand still tended to see Irene Moore through the doubtful eyes of an orphaned five-year-old. Since the day Irene had moved in, shortly after Rand's fifth birthday, she'd been good to him, but they had never clicked.

Suspecting the lack was his, he nevertheless always gave her his respect. At times like this, when despite the scandal Jasmine had caused, Irene's concern for Jasmine was evident, he couldn't be blind to her good side. If she made Jasmine more comfortable, he'd even have reason to thank her.

AT IRENE'S WELCOMING HUG, Jasmine tried to put her whirling thoughts in order. But it wasn't easy. Rand had implied the same person who had killed her father had tried to murder her. Her father had died in one fire, and she'd almost lost her life in another fire. Suspicions clouded her mind and fear tingled over her neck.

While Rand made introductions, Jasmine collected herself and studied the immaculately groomed blonde. After Rand's comments about her, Jasmine hadn't expected the woman to be warm or welcoming, but she'd been just that—the opposite of what he'd led her to believe. Had Rand lied? Or did he see Irene differently than Jasmine did?

Tall, thin and moving with a nervous energy that couldn't hide the swollen lids of her eyes and the dark shadows beneath, Irene looked as if she'd used makeup to cover the fact she'd not slept last night.

Jasmine guessed the woman had sobbed her eyes out. She was still a stunning woman who displayed a gracious charm that had to be inherent to her character. Jasmine could no more imagine this women setting fires to kill her and Talbot than she could her computer making illogical calculations.

Patting her neatly coiffed hair, Irene spoke in an elegant Southern drawl. "Don't tell me Rand has already put you to work in the family business?"

"I needed a job."

Irene rested a well-manicured hand on Rand's shoulder. "It's not fair of him to keep you to himself. And while you work, I suppose he's been telling you the family secrets."

Secrets? Jasmine's hopes of learning about the past rose. "Before I came here, had you ever heard of Lily Ross?"

"Never." Irene bit her bottom lip.

Was she telling the truth? Jasmine didn't know her well enough to guess. "I'm sorry if I'm making you uncomfortable. If you feel like talking, I'd love to hear about my father."

Irene's eyes filled with tears, and she tightened her grip on Rand's shoulder. "Talbot was a wonderful husband, a terrific father."

A lump formed in Jasmine's throat. "I wish I could have met him."

"We all loved him. But he wasn't a saint," Rand said dryly, pulling back from Irene's grasp.

"My Talbot didn't have one enemy," Irene insisted, her tone and stiff, erect posture daring him to contradict her.

But Irene was wrong. If Talbot had been murdered, he had at least one enemy. And now that same enemy might be after Jasmine. Irene and the rest of the family must be unaware of the other two fires Talbot was involved in. For some reason, Rand and Talbot must have kept their knowledge secret from the family. But why?

Before her father's death, had he suspected someone in his family might be trying to kill him? Talbot had confided in Rand. And died. She'd best be careful not to make the same mistake.

Jasmine caught Rand's eye and he shook his head slightly, silently warning her that Irene was unaware of his suspicions about Talbot's death. A sudden thought chilled Jasmine to the marrow of her bones. In mystery novels, wasn't the primary murder suspect always the spouse of the victim?

If the police considered her father's death accidental, they wouldn't have investigated Irene. Was the woman's grief an act, perhaps as good an act as what had seemed her sincere welcome?

The air conditioner cycled on, raising goose bumps on Jasmine's flesh. Irene noted her slight shudder and, diamond rings winking, reached out and took Jasmine's hand. "Why, dear, you're icy. Unfortunately Moore House doesn't have individual thermostats, and the boys do like the air cold. I'll make sure Belle puts extra blankets in your room. For now, let me find you a sweater."

"Please, don't trouble—"

"It's no trouble." Irene exited as quickly as she'd entered, her heels tapping a sharp staccato as she left her too-sweet scent and more questions than ever swirling in her wake.

Jasmine faced Rand, who was watching her reactions with keen interest, and wished she could read his thoughts. Although he'd given Irene the courtesy a stepson should, she'd sensed a coolness between them. Clearly Rand didn't have the affection for Irene that her eldest son did. Recalling T.J.'s adamant warning not to distress his mother, Jasmine flushed with guilt, knowing she'd done just that. "Did I upset her terribly with my questions about Talbot?"

"With Irene it's hard to tell. She's always been a very emotional woman."

"T.J. takes after her. He didn't want me around before. How will he react once he learns I've upset his mother?"

Rand shrugged. "Protecting his mother isn't the only reason he wants you to leave."

"Really?" Either T.J. had taken an instant dislike to her or Rand knew something she didn't.

"Talbot may have known he had a daughter."

A weak sensation in her knees made her thankful she was already sitting. She preferred to believe her father had been unaware of her existence rather than to think he'd ignored her. Nervously, she licked her lip. "Could you explain?"

Rand took a chair and straddled it, his face grim. "The wording of Talbot's will is odd."

"What do you mean?"

"Charles urged Talbot to make out a will, but Talbot refused. After the second fire, he wrote a will by himself, by hand. Belle, the maid and cook, and Robson, our once-a-week gardener, witnessed the draft. Since Talbot was of sound mind, the damned document's legal."

She frowned, wondering why he was nettled by that fact. "I don't understand what the will has to do with me."

"Among other odd provisions, the will divides Talbot's assets among his four children."

She cocked her head, trying to understand. "Irene receives nothing?"

"She's entitled to the interest of one trust, and she can live in the house for the rest of her life."

Jasmine didn't know much about wills, trusts, or how the wealthy conducted their affairs. So far, the arrangement sounded normal enough. "I still don't understand—"

Rand leaned forward, his eyes intense. "Don't you see? Talbot's will specifically states the assets must be divided among *four* children. Until today, he only had three direct heirs, T.J., Art and Blain. Talbot was my guardian, but he never adopted me."

Excitement sizzled through her. Was it possible her father had remembered her after a lifetime of ignoring her? Why would he suddenly acknowledge her? And in so puzzling a way?

Guilt and the thought of dying did strange things to people. Perhaps he'd tried to set things right to clear his conscience. But his gesture came too late. Money, however useful and welcome, could never compensate for the lack of parents. Shoving back the bitter disappointments of her lonely childhood, she looked at Rand. He, too, had grown up without parents. But he'd had her father.

And Rand had had three "brothers" to fight and play with. He'd had siblings to share his adolescence with. Double dates. Learning to drive. Shared secrets. She'd had Aunt Daisy—but living with an adult wasn't the same.

The next words had to be said, but she had difficulty since they caused her chest to tighten with hurt.

"Until I showed up, everyone must have assumed the fourth child...was you."

"I thought so. That specific provision caused innumerable arguments and almost led to a lawsuit." The sun slicing through the drapes emphasized his harsh cheekbones and stoic expression. "I'd already inherited half the business from my parents. If I inherit from Talbot, too, I'll own the majority of Sinclair and Moore stock."

Jasmine steeled herself to ask him what she had to know. "So if I inherit from my father, who has the most to lose?"

Rand stared straight into her eyes as if in challenge. "I do."

Chapter Four

Jasmine wished she could read Rand's stare, but even in the bright lights of the makeshift office, his thoughts remained closed to her. What mattered for her was the reason behind her father's final bequest. Was Rand the fourth child? Or had Talbot sought to make up for her mother's disappearance and his own failure to acknowledge her during his lifetime by naming *her* as a beneficiary in his will?

And what of the powerful man looming over her and assessing her with an intensity she found hard to match? Until she'd shown up, the family would have assumed the fourth child was Rand. Her inheriting a quarter share would usurp Rand's wealth and control of the company.

Simply put, he had an overpowering motive to want her out of the picture. Her heart slipped into her throat.

Rand's job offer could be a ruse to keep her nearby, within striking distance. He'd even mentioned he'd lived at Moore House twenty-five years ago during the time her mother had disappeared. Although he'd only been three years old, he might have remembered the name Ross through the intervening years. At Jasmine's appearance on his doorstep, he would have recognized how a fourth child could change the distribution of Talbot's assets.

If Rand had seen her mother's old letter, he could have tracked her down and set fire to her home. He could also have been the one who torched her father's cabin and boat and arranged the final "accident" that took his life. Rand had been so curious about the details of her fire. Had he wondered if he'd made any mistake and left a clue to his identity behind? As her doubts crystallized, uncertainty replaced her calm. She swallowed hard, but the bitter taste of suspicion lingered.

She recalled how he had held her close as he'd practically carried her into the hall, hands smoothing back her hair and caressing the wound on her wrist with tenderness. His touch had aroused a shimmering warmth deep inside her, reminding her how alone she was. Even with her doubts, a part of her hungered to know him better. Another part warned her to beware.

Could those same hands have struck the match that almost burned her alive? She had nothing but circumstantial evidence against him, but she couldn't take the chance of remaining with him in this house. Even while fright rose up to choke her, a vague perception of losing a chance at something precious saddened her.

His eyes didn't avoid hers, but they'd lost the warm glint of compassion. He hovered over her, his face hard as granite. Abruptly, his hand snaked out and his fingers handcuffed her wrist.

She tugged, but despite the additional strength from the fright shooting through her, she couldn't free her hand. She opened her mouth to scream.

He released her with an expression of disgust and shoved back his chair with vexation. Plunging his fingers into his hair, he gazed at her with pain-filled eyes. "To hell with being polite. You think I didn't guess you'd suspect me?"

His righteous anger stopped her scream mid-throat.

"I didn't burn down your house," he said urgently, in a sharp but low tone. "If I had, would I have told you about Talbot's will? Would I have offered you a job and invited you to live at Moore House?"

The logic of his argument slowly penetrated her hammering fear. Reminding herself that he would hardly kill her inside Moore House, she corralled her panicking thoughts. If he'd intended to kill her, he would have coaxed her into his car and driven her to an isolated spot, not asked the family attorney to help her. He wouldn't have told her about the will, either.

Remembering the Return-to-Sender stamp, she needed to know who at Moore House had refused her mother's letter, but she tucked the thought away, sensing now was not the time to voice more suspicions.

"I'm sorry," she said, forcing an apology through stiff lips. "I don't know you well, and I'm not sure who I can trust."

He nodded, a muscle tensing in his jaw. "I understand. However, I'm not the *only* one who would benefit if you aren't around to prove you're Talbot's daughter and the will stands up as we all agreed before you appeared."

Why was he helping her? Could she trust the information he so freely dispensed? Secreting her doubts in the back of her mind, she tried to keep the edginess out of her voice. "What do you mean?"

"Remember, I already own half the business, which I inherited from my parents. To avoid a court battle, instead of taking a quarter of Talbot's half share, I agreed to accept only one percent of Talbot's part of Sinclair and Moore."

As Rand settled against her desk, comprehension dawned. Rand wasn't greedy. But then he could afford to be generous, since he already owned half of Sinclair and Moore. Clearly he wanted majority control, and her half brothers had opted to give him an additional one percent of stock rather than go to court—an indication they trusted Rand's business acumen.

Her arrival had changed the established balance of power. Until she'd shown up, things had been settled. That extra one percent had still left Rand with majority control, fifty-one percent of the business. Staring down at her from his great height, he appeared anything but threatened. He observed her coolly, but she refused to let him intimidate her.

"So if I demand a full quarter share of Talbot's half of the business, my brothers would receive less."

"Exactly." His eyes gleamed approval that she'd caught on so quickly. She sensed his spark of interest in her as a woman, while suspecting him of an ulterior motive beyond having her within easy reach. She couldn't put her finger on his reason, but something besides a sexual tug-of-war was going on. It was almost as if he wanted her for another reason. As bait?

Had Rand asked her to stay to entice the arsonist into making a move toward her? Or maybe he thought there was a connection between her arsonist and Talbot's killer. Either way, her continued presence at Moore House would benefit him.

"There are other issues, too," he continued.

Her heart sank. Her thoughts were already spinning, and she wasn't sure how much more she could take. "Like?"

"Each of Talbot's sons controls different areas of the business. They all have their own agendas and may want to protect their territory." He cocked his head almost indulgently, then raised his eyebrow. "Blain, the youngest, rarely comes into the office, since he prefers playing beach volleyball to working. However, he likes his creature comforts and might not want his profits cut if you become a partner."

"And the others?"

"You've met T.J. As the oldest, he'll do whatever is necessary to protect the family."

"Go on." She kept her expression immobile. Did "whatever is necessary" include murder?

"Art, our accountant, is the peacemaker and sees himself as the voice of reason amid the chaos the rest of us create. But if you took a sudden interest in his books, he wouldn't be happy."

"You like them all, don't you?" Despite his earlier confrontation with T.J., she'd heard his tone soften when he'd spoken of her brothers. She wanted to see if he'd admit his feelings.

"We get on well enough. Then there's Charles, the corporate attorney, who's probably forgotten more about business than we'll ever know. Charles works exclusively for Sinclair and Moore. Any change in power could threaten his job. And you can't forget Irene. Your appearance will cause a scandal in her social circles."

By gaining a family, Jasmine had just complicated her simple life. No matter how riveting she found her new circumstances, she couldn't forget that someone had almost incinerated her while she slept. While the arsonist had failed to kill her, he'd done a damn fine job of placing her in an untenable situation.

If she wanted to stay alive, she had to figure out who was behind the fire. Fast.

Almost overwhelmed by Rand's information, she wasn't sure where to start looking for an arsonist. She considered running away. But where would she go? She didn't even know what or whom she was running from. And if she didn't stay and figure out who was after her, she'd spend the rest of her life looking over her shoulder. If her courage failed now, she'd always wonder whether she'd done everything she could do to discover what had happened to her mother. In addition, she'd lose the opportunity to meet her other brothers.

Besides, she wanted Rand's help. Facing her problems alone seemed daunting. But surely Rand's offer of assistance had strings attached. What did he want from her? And how much was she willing to give?

Jasmine tried to ignore the tension, strung tight as piano wire, arcing between them. She needed answers. "Who usually gets the mail?"

Rand folded his arms over his chest. "Wondering if I recognized your name, got your address from the envelope and burned down your house?"

Her stomach knotted into a hard ball. "Did you?"

"I can think of better things to do with a beautiful woman."

"That's great." She pretended not to hear the edge of desire in his voice. "But tell me who around here gets the mail?"

He shrugged. "Could have been anyone. And whoever carries it from the mailbox leaves the letters in the front hall. Everyone had equal access.''

Terrific.

She tried another angle. ''Tell me more about my brothers.''

Even after meeting T.J. and Irene and Charles, it was hard to comprehend she was part of the Moore family. Except for Aunt Daisy, most of her life she'd been alone.

Now she had brothers—at least, half brothers. Would Art and Blain resent her presence as T.J. seemed to or would they welcome her? A family added a new dimension to her life. If she stayed at Moore House, she'd become immersed in their daily lives, an opportunity almost impossible to resist. Would she grow close to her new family?

Her chest tightened. Was one of her brothers trying to kill her?

And what of Rand? He was more a part of this family than she, but whenever she brought up the topic of the Moores, his expression shut down and he refused to say much about them. It didn't take a psychologist to guess he liked her brothers. Was he thinking that one of them was a murderer and the possibility bothered him?

She no longer believed Rand would automatically inform her siblings, brothers she so desperately wanted to know and like, that she suspected someone in this house of arson. And yet, Rand kept his own thoughts about the family hidden.

Rand's face had transformed into an enigmatic mask at her request for more information about the Moores, and he spoke as if choosing his words carefully. ''I don't want to color your judgment about them with my opinions.'' He checked his watch. ''Why don't we hold off this discussion until after you've met everyone? In the meantime, there's someone you should talk to.''

RAND TOOK JASMINE to the first floor at the rear of the house. Unlike the rest of the mansion, the modernized cream-colored kitchen had a light and airy atmosphere. The scent of newly baked bread greeted them.

Belle stood over a gleaming granite island, rolling out dough for what looked like a piecrust. Flour dusted the cook's orange hair as she waved them over. ''Peach cobbler won't be ready for an hour.''

Rand filched a slice of fresh peach and held it to Jasmine's lips. Without thinking, she opened her mouth and reveled in the succulent sweetness.

Belle shook her rolling pin at Rand, but her eyes flared with amusement. ''None of that in my kitchen.''

''Yes, ma'am.'' Rand slung his arm over Belle's frail shoulders. ''When we were kids, she used to chase us out of here with the rolling pin.''

''Young scamps stole Mr. Moore's dinner once. Caught them feeding it to a neighbor's dog.''

Rand grimaced. ''It was liver.''

Jasmine watched the interplay between the old woman and Rand, feeling warmed by their camaraderie and glad he'd brought her here.

''How long have you worked for the Moores?'' Jasmine asked.

''Going on forty-two years now.'' The woman pulled away from Rand and returned to kneading her dough.

Jasmine propped her elbows on the counter. "So what was Rand like as a boy?"

Belle's eyes twinkled at Rand's obvious discomfiture. "Oh, he was mighty sad when he first came here. But he and Talbot hit it off right away. Later Rand stood up for the Moore kids—even when they done wrong."

"So defending the underdog comes naturally to him?"

Rand shook his head. "Ladies, surely you have other things to talk about than my past."

"None as fascinatin'." Belle winked at Jasmine. "Before the redevelopment, Rand was always draggin' the poor kids from down the street into my kitchen, askin' me to feed them a good meal. He still treats everyone good, even his employees."

Rand sighed in mock irritation. "Enough. Jasmine, didn't you have some questions to ask Belle?"

Jasmine nodded, surprised she'd needed reminding. Belle obviously cared for Rand. Was she being so friendly toward Jasmine since Rand approved of her? Or did she have her own agenda? "Ever meet a woman named Lily Ross?"

Belle shrugged, concentrating on her dough. "Might have. These boys bring home lots of lady friends."

"None as pretty as Jasmine." Rand's hot look raised her temperature a degree.

She told herself she was warm from the oven and scooted a stool closer to Belle. "I'm talking twenty-five to thirty years ago. Lily would have been seeing Talbot Moore, not one of his sons."

Rand took a seat beside her, crowding her. Was the curiosity in his blatant expression due to his noticing her sudden need to put distance between them? Was he wondering how she'd react next? Or was he simply interested in her questions?

Belle pounded the dough, her eyes avoiding Jasmine's. "What'd she look like?"

Pain stabbed Jasmine, and her heart ached. She'd lost every picture of her mother when her photo albums burned in the fire with the rest of her things. The precious picture of her mother wearing dangling silver earrings, a floppy hat and a wide smile was gone forever. Swallowing the lump in her throat, she forced a calm tone. "Lily was a few inches shorter than me—about five foot four. She had blond hair and blue eyes."

"Don't recall the mister datin' any blondes."

"Irene is blond," Jasmine pointed out.

Belle stubbornly refused to meet her gaze. "Her kind of blond comes out of a bottle. When she and the mister met, her hair was dark like T.J.'s and Art's. Blain must have gotten his fair colorin' and light hair from his grandmama."

"You've no recollection of Talbot dating Lily?" Rand asked.

Belle licked her bottom lip. "No."

She's lying. Or hiding something, Jasmine thought. But what? And why?

Rand's eyes bored into Belle, who refused to meet his gaze, also. Casually he swung his arm over Jasmine's shoulders as if showing the other woman he supported her fully. But Belle volunteered nothing.

Their questions weren't leading anywhere, so Jasmine tried another angle as she attempted to ignore Rand's disturbingly close presence and put out of her mind that her pulse had just doubled. "Did Talbot keep a diary?"

Rand snorted with amusement as he nabbed another slice of peach and popped it into his mouth. "I doubt it."

Belle shook her head.

"Are there any old scrapbooks or photo albums around?" Jasmine persisted.

Smoothing her dough into the pan, Belle deftly added peaches. Her eyes darted to the empty doorway, then down to the counter. "Maybe in the attic, but it's locked, and—" Belle paused, frowning in thought "—I don't think the attic key is with the others in the hall. Charles may have it."

Others in the hall? Recalling that someone may have stolen into her locked room while she slept, Jasmine made her voice casual. "Does anyone besides me have a key to my room?"

Rand looked at her with a gleam in his eyes that she had no trouble interpreting. Instead of following her line of questions, he was watching her lips hungrily, and clearly it wasn't peach cobbler that tempted him.

"We hang the room keys in the front hall," Belle said.

Great. Anyone could unlock her door with a key from the hallway without even bothering Charles.

Tonight she'd brace a chair under the doorknob. Her action wouldn't keep out a determined intruder— but at least she'd have warning if anyone tried to enter.

"Just one more question." Jasmine took her mother's letter out of her pocket and held it so Belle could easily see the stamp and handwriting. "Have you ever seen this before?"

"Nope. Never seen that letter in my life." Belle spun and placed the cobbler into the preheated oven, once again avoiding her gaze. The woman wasn't good at hiding her reactions. *Something* was bothering her.

AFTER WORKING THROUGH the afternoon, Rand still had to make a few phone calls in the upstairs office, but he'd suggested that Jasmine quit for the day. As she descended the dimly lit stairs, on the way to her room to freshen up before dinner, a silhouette emerged from the shadows a few steps from her room.

Her neck prickled. A man stepped out of the darkness into the light, a scowl of displeasure on his tight features. Jasmine's tightly held breath whooshed out in relief as she recognized T.J.

But his eyes burned with unbridled anger, impaling her with a fury fierce enough to send her fleeing in panic.

She gritted her teeth, fighting the trembling that seized her. She wouldn't cower. It wasn't her fault whose child she was or what her father had done.

"What did you say to my mother?" he demanded.

"Why?" She refused to be bullied, although her mouth was dry as sand.

T.J. advanced, the scowl deepening. He clenched and unclenched his fists. "She spent the afternoon in tears."

"I didn't—"

He slapped his fist into an open palm. "I warned you not to upset her. But you had to ask her questions about Lily Ross and Talbot, didn't you? Had to go poking your nose into business that doesn't concern you.''

''I merely—''

''You should leave Moore House. Now. You don't belong.''

She tried to edge by him in an attempt to reach her room. ''I have every right—''

He raised his arm, his palm thudding the wall and halting her progress. Detained close enough to him to feel the heat of his anger, she considered shouting for Rand.

T.J. glowered, his eyes pinning her, his face inches from hers. ''Get out of here while you still can.''

She opened her mouth to protest—but T.J. dropped his arm and brushed by. He'd disappeared downstairs before she collected herself enough to wonder what he'd meant by his terrifying last threat.

Collapsing against the wall, rattled by T.J.'s animosity, she wished Rand was there to hold her. His strong arms would be a great comfort in this house of strangers.

The emotional aftermath of her argument with T.J. left her weak, uncertain and dizzy. Was this how families acted? Accusing one another. Bullying their physically weaker siblings. Interrupting before she could get a word in edgewise. Too bad she hadn't realized sooner. She wouldn't have wasted all those years envying her friends.

Swelling fear exhausted her emotionally and physically. Although T.J. hadn't touched her, Jasmine felt battered and more vulnerable and frightened than she wanted to admit. Dragging herself the last few steps to her room, she knew what she must do.

Tonight she'd tell Rand she was leaving. Accepting his job offer had been iffy from the start. But with T.J.'s hostility and his clear warning, she wasn't about to stick around and discover whether her eldest half brother intended to follow through on his threat or was merely bluffing.

If all her brothers shared T.J.'s attitude, facing them wasn't something she longed to do—even if she could count on Rand's support. Better to leave before anger exploded into physical violence.

Shaking with irritation, frustration and a little bit of guilt, Jasmine stopped in front of her door. Had she really upset Irene so badly? Or had the woman used the excuse to complain to her son, hoping to rid herself of an unwanted houseguest?

Unsure what to think, Jasmine opened her bedroom door and gasped in surprise.

New clothing lay stacked along one side of her bed. Dresses hung in the open closet. She hadn't asked Rand to have someone shop for her. With her limited savings, she could make do until the insurance company settled her claim. She didn't need charity. Well, the items could be returned. And she wouldn't put up with T.J.'s anger. Leaving Moore House would be best.

Shoving aside the last of her uneasiness, she forced herself to think about her immediate future. Sinking onto the bed, she checked her watch, determined to get out quickly. Unfortunately she'd been so caught up in Rand's charm, the Moore family and her past, she'd neglected to take care of business details she normally would never have overlooked.

Picking up the phone and dialing, she fought to

keep her voice steady as she asked to speak with her insurance agent. "Mr. Kramer, please."

"Kramer speaking."

"This is Jasmine Ross. My house burned down the night before last. I want to know if my claim's been settled and when I can expect reimbursement."

Secretly she hoped to have a check in hand tomorrow, but could wait a week if necessary.

Kramer cleared his throat. "Let me see. Even if the claim hasn't been settled yet, most policies have a clause that disperses funds for temporary housing. Let me pull up your policy."

There was a very long pause.

"Is something wrong?" Jasmine asked, betraying none of the residual turmoil swirling in her head.

"I'm afraid so. Apparently the fire department's investigation turned up evidence of arson."

She sighed, frustrated with bureaucracy, wondering how long it would take to straighten out her life. "I already told the police about the possibility of arson yesterday."

"The gasoline can found beside you on the grass was wiped clean of fingerprints, and that's definitely suspicious."

Her heart started to pound. She'd hoped the investigators would find evidence that would point to the arsonist. Instead, Kramer seemed to be implying she had more problems than she'd thought.

"Under the circumstances, we can't release any funds."

"I have to rebuild my business. And I'll have to refund the fall semester's tuition to my students." Her words fell on unsympathetic ears as Kramer said a fast goodbye.

Panic sent her pulse racing. What would she live on in the meantime? She had a few hundred dollars in the bank. If she was forced to reside in hotels, she'd exhaust her resources within a week.

She was homeless, almost broke. Without collateral, the bank wouldn't issue her a loan. The air in the bedroom closed in. The dark walls, eerily somber, seemed to be suffocating her.

Breathe.

Forcing in air, she stared at herself in the old Victorian mirror, barely recognizing herself. The vital woman of yesterday had been replaced by a hollow-cheeked waif. A waxy pallor had erased the normal glow of her cheeks, and darkness haunted her eyes.

What was she going to do? She fought the feelings of despair engulfing her. Waiting at Moore House for either the insurance money or her inheritance was out of the question. The arson investigation might never be solved, and for a will to clear probate took months. With T.J.'s threat hanging over her, she had to leave Moore House and find another job before Rand could discover her plans and talk her out of going.

Grabbing up her backpack, she stuffed in a shirt, slacks, underwear and her mother's music box. Now that she'd decided to leave, she must hurry. No doubt if Rand caught her, he'd use his persuasive charm to sway her, and right now, in her shaky condition, she wasn't up to arguing with anyone, never mind a man as irresistible as Rand Sinclair.

She refused to owe him and would write a check to repay him for the items she took. Rushing to the dresser, she grabbed a toothbrush and a hairbrush and stuffed them into the backpack.

A loose sheet of unfamiliar cream paper fell from

the dresser onto the floor. With a dreadful feeling in her heart, she leaned over and slowly read the words scribbled in bold black letters; "Your mother is alive. But there's danger. Don't trust anyone."

Chapter Five

Joy that Lily might be alive warred with Jasmine's need to escape Moore House and nebulous danger. Rereading the warning in the note, Jasmine warily looked around her bedroom. Anyone could have come into her room while she'd been working with Rand—Irene when she'd gone to fetch her a sweater, Belle during her round of cleaning, or Rand's secretary, who had delivered the clothing—even Charles or one of her brothers.

Jasmine had been with Rand all day, but he could have slipped the note into her room before he joined her for breakfast and argued with T.J. For whatever reason, Rand wanted her to stay—so the probability of his leaving the note was low.

The eerie sound of mocking laughter suddenly invaded the room.

Jasmine sprinted down the dark hall and around the corner. She knocked into something hard. *Someone* hard.

She screamed.

Large hands clamped on her waist. "Take it easy."

It took an instant for Rand's warm voice to penetrate her panic, for her to comprehend that she'd run, not into danger, but to safety. She plastered herself to his shirtfront, grateful it was him.

He wrapped her in his embrace, pulling her closer. "Hey, what's wrong?"

For a moment she reveled in the pleasure of his warmth, yielded to his strength, surrendered to the feeling of safety his arms provided. Clinging to his broad shoulders, delighting in the crisp hair in the open V of his shirt against her cheek, she didn't ever want to let go.

"Someone was in my room."

His powerful body went rigid. "Who?"

"I don't know. But T.J. threatened me. Then I found a warning note. And someone was laughing at me."

He smoothed her hair off her forehead, apparently dumbfounded. "Whoa. Slow down. You aren't making sense."

She fought for control, settling her hands on his chest. "T.J. was angry that I'd upset Irene. He told me to leave while I still could." She shuddered, remembering the hostility in her brother's eyes, his barely checked rage.

Rand's muscles bunched beneath her fingers. "If he hurt you—"

"He didn't. But he wants me to leave." She took a deep, steadying breath. "And I was going. I'd packed a bag and that's when I found a note."

"Let me see."

"I left it in my room." As much as she wanted Rand to hear the evil laughter in her room, she didn't like the idea of returning. Had the sound been a figment of her imagination? She was under considerable stress. But she'd just checked the room and found it empty mere minutes before the laughter began.

Rand released her, tugged her around the corner and down the hall toward her room. "Come on. Show me the note."

Missing the security of his embrace, she followed him into her room, walked around the bed and pointed. "It's right..."

The note was gone! And so was the mocking laughter.

Jasmine could feel the blood draining from her face. She swayed in shock. Rand caught her and eased her over to the empty side of the bed.

"The note was right there," she insisted weakly. "It fell from the dresser onto the floor, and I left it there."

Puzzlement furrowed Rand's brow. He got down on hands and knees. "Maybe a draft blew it under the bed."

She leaned over the edge, watching him. "Don't touch it except on the edges. That way, the police might find fingerprints."

His questioning gaze riveted on her. "There's nothing here."

"But—" Ignoring her dizziness, she climbed down and looked. Rand was correct. Damn it—why hadn't she kept the note?

Because she'd dropped it when she'd heard the laughter and run. Jasmine stood, went to the shoe boxes and looked beneath each one. She picked the clothing up from the bed, checking between their folds. She searched under the bureau and in the closet.

Rand must think her a fool. Or insane. But if she was seeing and hearing things, she *was* crazy. If she wasn't careful, her new family might have her committed.

Finally, with nowhere else to look, she faced him. "Someone must have slipped into the room and taken the note while I was with you on the landing."

Rand took her icy hand and rubbed warmth into her. "It's a possibility."

Her heart warmed that he seemed to believe her. "I thought someone had come into my room last night while I was asleep. But this morning I'd convinced myself it was my imagination. Now I'm not so sure."

"Describe the note to me. Don't leave out any detail, no matter how small."

"The paper was cream, rich looking. The only writing was block letters written by a black marker."

"What did the note say?" Rand asked gently.

Jasmine hesitated. Should she tell him the note had stated that her mother was alive? No matter how sympathetic Rand sounded, she must have already stretched her credibility to the utmost. If she told him the missing note mentioned a mother who'd disappeared twenty-five years ago, he might think she'd gone off the deep end. Now wasn't the time to confide when she hadn't had a chance to consider the note's ramifications herself.

Little tingles of hope that her mother might still be alive made her cautious. "The message read, 'Danger. Don't trust anyone.'"

Rand tilted up her chin with his hand. His stormy gray eyes locked onto hers, and he lowered his tone to a husky murmur. "I won't let anyone hurt you."

His mouth was less than an inch from hers. Slowly

he dipped his head, making his intention clear. He was going to kiss her unless she pulled back.

His look was so tender, she expected his kiss to be gentle. She was wrong.

His mouth swooped down on her hungrily, taking her in a haze of sensual passion. His arms, like steel chains, locked her tight to his chest, and the electricity of his powerful body jolted through her.

Overwhelmed by the sudden fire curling in her belly and radiating downward, she rose up on her toes, kissing him with a fervor she'd never known. She wound her arms around his neck, threaded her fingers into his thick hair and tugged him closer, captivated by his musky male essence scented with a spicy balsam cologne.

He tasted of sparkling ambrosia, flavored with a hint of cinnamon and wine. Skin prickling pleasurably, heart pounding lustfully, she returned his kiss.

She reveled in the delicious sensations as he whetted her appetite for sustenance she hadn't known she'd needed. He slipped his hand beneath her shirt and teasingly skimmed upward.

"Ahem." A young man in the doorway cleared his throat.

Jasmine jerked away, her cheeks flushing with embarrassment. Rand, seemingly not the slightest bit ruffled, turned to face the intruder.

Jasmine had no doubt the stranger was another of her brothers. His facial features resembled T.J.'s but weren't quite as sharp. Lacking T.J.'s simmering anger, this brother's eyes were both concerned and amused at the intimate scene he'd interrupted.

"I was in the kitchen and thought I heard someone

scream.'' He looked from Rand to her. "Everything all right?''

Rand took her hand and led her toward her brother. "Jasmine, this is Art, Irene and Talbot's middle son.''

"Welcome to the family,'' Art said, his face open and friendly. "Was that you I heard scream?''

Jasmine nodded sheepishly. "I bumped into Rand.''

Art chuckled, his eyes lit with mirth. "Well, he's big enough to frighten anyone.''

Rand scowled. "How long have you been home?''

Art's smile faded. "Long enough to calm down T.J. and pour black coffee into Blain. I left Charles attempting to sober him up. Then I went to see Mother. She's not coping well. Perhaps you could talk some sense into her?''

"Would you excuse us?'' Rand asked Jasmine.

"I won't keep him long.'' Art clamped one arm on Rand's shoulder and led him from the room, leaving Jasmine alone.

She liked this brother. Unlike T.J., with his hot temper, Art seemed to be even-tempered, honest and pleasant. She could no more imagine him sneaking into her room for malicious purposes than she could Rand.

Discovering that one of her brothers wasn't hostile caused her to rethink her decision to leave. Her finances were so meager, it limited her choices. Determined not to let the searing kiss she and Rand had just shared influence her, she refused to dwell on her swollen lips and the blood still singing through her, heating her with an excitement she couldn't squelch. Yet, she must put aside her infatuation with Rand and think.

So much had happened, setting her thoughts in order was difficult. From the first moment she'd stepped into Moore House, her senses had been confused. She'd heard loud male voices arguing, but Rand had denied anyone was with him. Last night, someone had seemingly stolen into her room, but after she'd turned on the light, she'd found herself alone. And she *had* seen that note—damn it. But she and Rand had searched the room thoroughly without finding one sheet of cream-colored paper. Earlier, mocking laughter had sent her fleeing from her room.

She shivered, wondering if the old house had ghosts. Although she didn't believe in such nonsense, paranormal phenomenon beat the scary alternative that she was seeing and hearing things that weren't there.

Never before had she questioned her sanity. She furiously shoved the thought aside.

She wasn't crazy.

She *wasn't*.

She was so tired, maybe she'd been daydreaming. No matter how unpleasant and frightening her thoughts, she had to face them. Was stress causing hallucinations? Could she have been drugged? Or was she losing her mind? The possibilities chilled her.

If someone was playing tricks on her, she was just as sane as the trickster. But she had to be smarter.

Recalling the note's warning of danger, she fought down renewed fright. Had she really seen that sheet of paper? Or had her overtaxed mind conjured up an excuse to go running into Rand's arms?

The note had seemed so real. But if it *was* real, what had happened to it?

Deciding there was no point to doubting her sanity

or she'd never make sense of her circumstances, she thrust back the unpleasant thought. Two things stood out in her mind. The note that said her mother was still alive. And T.J.'s threat.

Uncomfortable without enough information to make an informed decision whether to stay or go, she mulled over her options. Remaining in the house where she would see and work with Rand every day held a certain appeal, but satisfying her curiosity about Rand wasn't worth putting her life at risk.

Searching for her mother was another matter. She'd never be able to live with herself if she walked away from the prospect of finding answers to the twenty-five-year-old mystery. Staying another few days *was* worth the risk of learning whether her mother was really alive—or the note only a cruel hoax. Jasmine might be in danger, but Rand had promised to protect her.

Even if she fled halfway across the country, her life still could be in danger. She could do nothing to prevent someone from following. At least here, Rand would help and she had a chance to search for her mother.

The clues to her mother's whereabouts were probably right here in the house, in the memories of Irene, Charles and Belle. Even her brothers and Rand might recall important information if she asked the right questions.

Weighing everything against the possibility of finding her mother, she reached her decision. She had to stay. For now, Moore House was the best place to unravel her past and secure her future.

AFTER DINNER AND COFFEE in the dining room, where everyone but a hungover Blain had gathered around the large table, Jasmine, restless to search the attic in hopes of learning more about Talbot and her mother, asked Charles for the key.

Irene wrinkled her nose. "Why ever would you want to go up there?"

"She's poking her nose where it doesn't belong," T.J. muttered.

Rand glared at T.J., who refused to meet his gaze.

Art sent Jasmine an apologetic shrug. "Now, T.J., I thought we agreed not to blame Jasmine for circumstances beyond her—"

"*We* agreed on nothing." T.J.'s eyes darkened. "You—"

"That's enough." Rand threw down his napkin in obvious disgust, then turned to Jasmine with a neutral look. "I've a few reports to read. After Charles gives you the key, I'll help search for the old photo albums. You might want to change first. There's bound to be a few old cobwebs up there."

"Not to mention dust, spiders and cockroaches," T.J. said meanly.

Irene frowned. "I do not have cockroaches in my house."

"Of course not, Mother," Art agreed, obviously trying to keep peace.

Mollified, Irene patted her hair and pasted a bright smile on her face. "But perhaps I should have Belle mop, dust and vacuum—"

"Mother," Art argued, his patience clearly waning, "cleaning would be impossible unless you throw out all the old furniture, pictures, clothing and knick-knacks you've collected over the last decades."

"Whatever." Irene stared into her empty coffee cup, seeming to have lost interest in the subject.

Art was consoling her as Rand left the dining room. Charles led Jasmine into the study, a kindly smile on his face. "Are you feeling all right, dear?"

"Sure. Why do you ask?" Did the strain of the past hours show on her face?

"You looked pale during dinner. Is anything bothering you?"

Jasmine thought him kind to notice and ask. "I'm just not accustomed to family discussions. I suppose it'll take some time to get used to Moore House."

"Well, if there's anything at all I can do to help, don't hesitate to ask." He puttered around in the top drawer of the desk he and Rand shared and finally pulled out a skeleton key. "Here, you go, dear."

"Thanks." Jasmine slipped the key into the pocket of her sweater.

"Don't lose it. While a locksmith can copy a skeleton key, we can't make a duplicate at the local hardware store."

"I'll be careful," she promised, surmising some of the stored antiques in the attic were valuable and glad he trusted her with the key. "Do you have any idea if there might be some old photographs in the attic? I was hoping to find pictures of Talbot."

"His picture's in the hall downstairs."

She expelled an impatient sigh. "I've missed so much of his life. I wanted to see his likeness as a child, pictures of his parents—my grandparents. And pictures when Talbot was a young man."

"Are you looking for a picture of him with your mother?" Charles asked perceptively, his wrinkled face scrunching in a kindly smile.

Hope fluttered in her chest. "Have you ever seen one?"

"Can't say that I have, dear." Before disappointment rocked her, Charles put a friendly arm over her shoulder and walked her from the study. "There's a green military chest up there somewhere. That would be the place to start. Come on, I'll show you."

"But Rand said—"

"This old house has several attic entrances." Charles passed his palm over the bald spot on his head. "I'll just point out which entrance is closest to the chest. Then you'll know where to bring Rand."

They climbed to the second-story landing where she'd normally turn to go to her room. But Charles headed up the flight of stairs that led near to the room Rand used for his office. Instead of turning right, Charles led her to the left, walking over slick floor tiles that had been varnished, the grout yellowed with age. Wallpaper, the design stubby and ill proportioned in an ugly shade of brownish gray, darkened the narrow hall. Dim lighting left murky shadows in the corners.

Up ahead, two bronze figures on marble bases bracketed a door. Charles huffed, his breath coming in wheezes. "Here we are."

Jasmine flinched as an electronic racket filled the air. Charles reached into his pocket and retrieved his beeper. He squinted at the message. "Just leave the key in the lock. If you enter through there, you should find Talbot's chest. I've got to get to a phone. Please, excuse me."

The older man hurried off, and Jasmine hoped he would be all right after he'd gone to the trouble of bringing her up here. She didn't like the sound of his labored breathing. Climbing two flights of stairs so quickly hadn't been easy for him.

She stared at the unlocked door and withdrew the key from her pocket, wanting one quick look before returning to change clothes and find Rand. With a flick of her wrist, she turned the key and the knob, threw back the door and peered inside. She'd expected to find the attic—but another staircase led upward. Craning her neck, she could just make out a dark green chest at the top of the stairs.

A prickling sensation of being watched teased her. She glanced back over her shoulder, then up ahead. After receiving the note warning of danger, she wouldn't go into the dark attic without Rand. Leaving the door open, Jasmine went to change and find Rand.

After donning jeans and a T-shirt, she met Rand in his bedroom next door. He sat in a wing chair, frowning over a report. Piles of papers spilled atop the desk, overflowed onto the floor and formed a sea of chaos in the otherwise well-appointed room. With a bed, armoire and dressing bureau, the plain bedroom had an unadorned look, lacking personal items that would have indicated Rand's interests and hobbies. Except for the piles of papers, this room was no more *his* than a stranger's.

"Come in," he said, without looking up from his reading.

Scooting around the papers, she took the only empty seat available, the edge of his bed. Rand didn't notice. He rubbed his chin in his palm, his elbow resting on the arm of the chair, his dark eyebrows drawing into a frown.

"Is something wrong?" she asked hesitantly.

Rand put down the papers with a shrug. Damn

right, there was something wrong. He'd been reading profit-and-loss statements for too long not to notice the company's expenses were running over budget. "Tomorrow, I want to go over the expense reports on our biggest jobs. Some of these numbers seem too high."

"Okay."

She sat on the edge of his bed, as if she thought he might pounce. Was she that afraid of him? Not that he hadn't considered the prospect of what she'd look like in his bed, welcoming him with a sparkling twinkle in her eyes. From their one kiss, he had learned she was incredibly passionate, even if she was doing her best to appear prim and proper right now.

Several tendrils of blond hair had escaped her top-knot, framing her delicately featured face. Her too-wide eyes looked haunted with uncertainties. He only wished he had some answers. For her. For him. The sooner he got to the bottom of his investigation, the better off they'd all be.

He stood and approached her, knowing his nearness made her uneasy. "I called the secretary who shopped for and delivered the clothing to your room."

She twisted her hands in her lap. Then, as if realizing she was revealing a weakness, she tucked her fingers beneath her thighs. "Why? You don't believe me about the note?"

"I believe you."

Her heavily lashed lids opened wide. "Why?"

Rand couldn't tell her the truth. He couldn't voice his suspicions, either. She was hiding something from him about the note. He was sure of it. And after she'd cried out in her first words of panic that someone had been laughing at her, she'd neglected to mention that little tidbit again—a curious omission.

He held out his hand to her. "I have no reason not to believe you. Why would you lie?"

When she placed her smooth hand in his, his heart jerked at the relief in her eyes. The urge to take her into his arms and kiss her again was almost unbearable. Just by entering his bedroom, she'd raised his temperature until he'd had difficulty concentrating on much else besides maneuvering her into another embrace. If their second kiss was half as fiery as their first, the tempting convenience of tumbling her into his bed would be irresistible.

Not even Talbot's disapproval could stop Rand from wanting his daughter. He found Jasmine too appealing, her combination of fragility and strength, exciting. Only the fact that he'd knowingly lied to her helped him rein in his emotions. Because when she found out what he had done, she would be furious.

The lies would always stand between them, and no solid relationship could be built on deception. There was no point seducing her only to have her spurn him later. No way would he set himself up for the kind of heartache his friend Dylan suffered since his lover deserted him. If Rand was smart, and he was, he would keep an emotional distance.

Kissing her might have been a mistake, but even if he could never have more, he'd never regret tasting her, holding her, breathing in her provocative scent. He'd thoroughly enjoyed her soft body pressed to his. Working with Jasmine every day was going to be torture. But he looked forward to their work in his office with an eagerness that surprised him.

He no longer attempted to think of Jasmine Ross

as an employee. Charles had already confirmed she would someday become his business partner unless someone in the family tried to fight her claim that she was Talbot's daughter. Her toppling the balance of power at Moore and Sinclair would have interesting possibilities—especially once he persuaded her to see things his way.

Even now as she took his hand, she looked at him as if weighing his intentions, probably wondering what he was hiding and why he believed her when he couldn't offer a logical reason. Although he had no proof of the note's existence, he believed Jasmine. Call it intuition, a hunch or the unconscious mind processing information he couldn't rationalize, his instincts told him she'd spoken the truth.

He squeezed her hand to encourage her. "Let's go see what's inside that chest."

"Charles showed me the door near your upstairs office."

Pleased that she held his hand as they climbed the stairs, he wondered what else she'd let him do. She hadn't objected to his kiss or his hand beneath her blouse. If Art hadn't interrupted, they might have wound up making passionate love.

Recalling her endearing blush at Art's entrance, he realized she would have been mortified if Art had walked in a few moments later instead. While the lady aroused him to white-hot readiness, she had some old-fashioned values he also appreciated.

They reached the third floor, and she released his hand so they could walk single file in the narrow hallway. Flipping on the light switch, he saw that two of the three bulbs were burnt out, and he made a mental note to have them replaced.

At the door to the attic, he held out his hand, palm up, behind him. "Give me the key."

"I left it in the lock."

He turned sideways. She peered past him. The door was closed. The key was gone.

Chapter Six

With a gasp, Jasmine reached for the knob and yanked. "Who locked the door?"

Rand studied her face, the warmth in his eyes belying the hard set of his jaw. "You sure you didn't—"

"I left the door open with the key in it," she insisted, heat flushing her cheeks. "I'm positive."

But was she? Doubt and despair assaulted her. She searched the floor, thinking the key might have fallen. But it wasn't in sight. Had she locked the door and taken the key? She dug her fingers into her pocket. It was empty.

Rand eyed her for a long, tension filled moment, then a lazy smile lifted the corners of his mouth. "Then someone took the key and locked the door," he suggested reasonably. "Maybe Belle?"

When he took her at her word, Jasmine was filled with gratitude. But while he seemed satisfied with his deduction, she wasn't so ready to accept his explanation. From her burned-down house, to Rand's blazing kiss, to the warning note branded into her memory, too much had happened lately that she couldn't explain.

Was she losing her mind? She closed her eyes for an instant, her thoughts spinning. The repeated incidents had to be more than forgetfulness. With an anguished heart, she considered the frightening possibility of mental illness. She recognized some of the symptoms in her behavior. Forgetfulness. Paranoia. Hallucinations. Perhaps she should talk to a doctor. But she dreaded a diagnosis. Fear had her doubting her senses, what she saw, what she heard, what she remembered.

Although she couldn't explain how the key and the warning note had disappeared, she vowed to search for answers. It seemed almost as if someone was following her around the house. But why? And how? She hadn't passed anyone in the narrow hallway on her way downstairs. But as Rand had pointed out, anyone could have closed and locked the door since she'd left the key in the lock.

Uneasy disappointment hit her. She'd been looking forward to opening the trunk and searching into her father's past. And if her mother was somehow alive, Jasmine hoped to uncover clues to find her. Every time she thought she was on the right trail, obstacles arose in her path, creating frustrating setbacks.

In retrospect, she wished she hadn't asked Charles about the attic key in front of the entire family. In the future, she would be more secretive, more selective in whom she confided.

"Let's ask Belle if she locked the door and took the key," Rand suggested.

"And if she didn't?" Or if she denied it? Jasmine wondered, remembering Belle's evasiveness. "Then what?"

"We'll ask everyone."

Rand's easy acceptance of her word bothered her almost as much as the missing key and locked door. His attitude didn't seem patronizing, but unless he was the culprit, he had no reason to believe her.

If she *was* sane, it was almost as if someone was trying to make her appear unbalanced with stupid pranks. A shudder shook her. Burning down her house had been no prank—she'd almost died.

She'd been counting on Rand's help while she looked into the mystery of her mother's disappearance and the possibility of finding her alive. But could she trust him?

Her heart said yes. But the note had warned her not to trust anyone, leaving her with a troubled feeling.

Ten minutes later, they'd spoken to almost everyone. No one admitted locking the door or having the key.

Rand led her to a bedroom at the back of the house. "That leaves Blain."

At last she would meet her youngest half brother. Rand knocked on the door but no one answered. Next, he pounded. When no one responded, Rand peeked inside.

Blain snored away so soundly in his messy bedroom, he didn't wake even when Rand shook his shoulder. Though unable to introduce herself to her youngest brother, she was impressed by his handsome appearance. Blain had long, sun-bleached blond hair that framed a surfer tan. Asleep without his shirt, the top button of his jeans unfastened, he sported the washboard abs of an athlete and the petulant lips of a child.

Rand drew the covers over Blain, a taut smile tugging at the corner of his mouth. "He's twenty-two, going on fourteen. He spends most of his time playing volleyball on Dolphin Beach."

While Rand didn't seem to resent Blain's life-style, she wondered how he could not. Rand obviously worked hard at the family business. So did T.J. and Art. Jasmine had no trouble imagining this youngest brother pouting until he got his way. Irene had probably spoiled him rotten. And with his good looks, she imagined the beach babes did the same.

There didn't appear to be an iota of malice in him asleep. But she had trouble believing any of the Moore household capable of murder—even T.J. who, although enraged, seemed direct and forthright rather than a sneaky coward who'd burn down a woman's house while she slept. Speculating about everyone's motives in her new family caused an uncomfortable dryness in her throat. Glad she had Rand to help her through this awkward time, Jasmine allowed him to lead her out of Blain's room.

They hadn't found the key. But either someone here was responsible for its disappearance and the locked attic door or she was losing her mind. Fear and doubts might be disrupting her memory and judgment. She'd thought she'd be able to tough it out, but she hadn't expected so much to be thrown at her. If she got out of the house, maybe she could think clearly. She'd do anything to keep her sanity. And if that meant running, she would run far from here and Rand.

Returning to her room to pack, she opened her door, dreading the attempt Rand would make to convince her to stay. He would protest vehemently. Saying no to him wouldn't be easy. Saying no to him might be the hardest thing she'd ever done.

She preceded him into the room. And stopped cold, shocked speechless, her feet frozen to the floor. In the dresser mirror, she saw Rand's reflection. His frown, quickly hidden, stabbed her.

Her mother's music box sat on the wide dressing table. On top of the music box lay the missing key.

HER EYES STINGING with unshed tears, her heartbeat speeding wildly, Jasmine sank onto the bed, unable to support herself on wobbly legs. She opened her mouth to protest that she hadn't left the key in this room, then thought better of it. Knowing the course these discussions usually took and how Rand reassured her she had nothing to fear, she was loathe to go to him for comfort and reassurance. But, oh, how she wished she could.

Handling shock after shock must have lowered her resistance to him. Never before had she required the security of a man's arms. Then again, never before had she been faced with the turmoil that now threatened to spin her into another dimension.

She needed Rand's arms around her. She ached to tug him beside her, run her fingers through his hair and breathe in his reassuring male scent.

No. She was no dependent, clinging female. She must deal with her problems alone. Instead of reaching out to him, she grabbed her pillow and hugged it to her stomach.

Rand's kisses, no matter how exciting, were not an answer to her difficulties. In fact, her attraction to him only complicated the issue. Could Rand deliberately be trying to distract her from the dangers at Moore House?

She curled tighter to her pillow, pressing her legs together, ignoring Rand altogether. Oh, God, what was happening to her? If only she felt more equal to the task of sorting through the tangle of deceptions and lies. She was weary of doubting the motives of everyone she met, exhausted by the constant undercurrent of unrest in this strange house. Her frayed nerves felt ready to snap from emotional overload, and a headache pounded her temples.

As if sensing her thoughts, Rand took a seat on the edge of her bed, careful not to touch her. "I don't know what to say."

There *was* nothing to say. Either she was nuts or someone was stalking her every move, setting her up to appear crazy—or attempting to drive her mad.

"I'd like to be alone." Her voice was tight, holding back a sob of frustration.

Rand lifted a hand, then dropped it back to his thigh. "Staying by yourself is a mistake."

Didn't he trust her since the missing key had turned up in her room? Furious, she lashed out at him. "It's *my* mistake to make. Please, just go."

"So you can finish packing and run away?"

"If I choose." She tossed a tendril of hair from her face and lifted her chin in defiance.

Rand reached out and skimmed his fingers over her arm, the gentle gesture in fierce contrast to the ruthlessness of his words. "I won't let you go."

His harsh counterattack knocked the air from her lungs. She jerked her arm from his caress in outrage, a quiver of fear stabbing her heart. With his jaw cocked at a severe angle, his shoulders stiff with determination, he clearly meant every word. Had she waited too long to leave? Would Rand keep her trapped, a prisoner, in this creepy mansion until she really did go insane?

"What did you say?"

"You heard me." His voice shifted subtly lower. "You aren't going anywhere."

"Irene already has one scandal to deal with. I imagine she won't be too pleased to learn you imprison women—"

"Woman." His gaze was potent, dangerous and supremely male. "One woman. Just you."

At the intimacy of his tone, Jasmine's temper swirled through her like rising steam, heating her blood as well as her face. "You can't keep me here against—"

"I can."

Flinging the pillow aside, she faced him. His gray eyes had darkened to a shocking, vibrant black. A black that could freeze granite with anger. A dangerous black that haunted, compelled and fascinated her.

She shoved away her treacherous thoughts and rose to her feet. She could argue with him for hours and never win. "Before I came to Moore House, I trusted what I saw, heard and felt."

"You can still believe in yourself. I do."

He didn't understand. He couldn't know what it was like for her to doubt her sanity. She could explain away or ignore a few strange incidents, but more was going on here. The idea of sleeping in this house had become out of the question. She had to fight not to hyperventilate. "I've had enough. Call me a coward, but I can't live like this anymore. I'm packing, and if you try to stop me, I'll—"

"You're in danger."

"That's why I'm leaving." Although searching the attic for clues about her mother tempted her, she wasn't about to risk staying in Rand's intoxicating presence another second.

Angling his head toward her, Rand cupped his fingers along her chin, tracing her lower lip with the pad of his thumb, stroking the middle until she licked the spot. He had the oddest effect on her, and resisting it called for extreme measures. Her mind said to run fast and far before he ensnared more than her chin. Her mind said not to listen to another word he said. Her mind said her heart was in danger.

His knuckles grazed her jawline, and his other hand cradled her cheek until she caught herself leaning into his touch and snapped upright. But as his fingers wound into her hair, his stroking allowed no escape.

She ached to throw herself into his arms and let him distract her with passion. She wanted answers to why she couldn't get him out of her mind. Although she had no explanation besides insanity for the direction her thoughts kept taking, she couldn't rid herself of the heady feminine power rushing through her with each choppy breath she drew.

All her problems ceased to exist. Thoughts of undressing Rand and making passionate love in the four-poster bed made her blood dance and her heart sing. She wasn't a flirt or a tease, and in another moment she'd be embarrassing herself by giving in to his artful seduction.

What was happening to her? Her senses had heightened. His clean scent taunted her, his husky tone shimmied down her spine and into her limbs. Her breasts tingled and ached for his caress.

When he tugged her to his chest and she sighed in contentment, she knew she had lost her mind. Then he was nibbling on her lips. And she couldn't think at all.

"We...can...only...find out the truth," he whispered between kisses, "if...you...stay with me."

He wrapped her in a possessive embrace. Heat radiated off his skin, warming the chill that had invaded her bones.

She lifted her chin and gazed into his eyes, searching for the truth. "How do I know you aren't taking advantage of a crazy lady?"

"You don't." He inclined his head at a mocking angle. "But you aren't crazy."

"How can you be so sure?"

"Haven't you noticed that nothing strange ever happens unless you're alone?" He paused while his fingers stroked lazy circles on her neck. His touch—and his stunning statement of his belief in her—held her spellbound. "But I want no misunderstandings between us. I want you. I've wanted you since the moment I saw you."

"Really?" His insistence that she stay had given her no chance to flee, no chance of retreat. He'd done no more than kiss her and she'd gone to him willingly. The flurried beat of her heart had rocketed her pulse rate to aerobic levels without her flexing a muscle. Never in her life had she been so mesmerized by a man or wanted to be held so badly.

"Oh, yes." His hand lifted to her topknot. "I've wanted to loosen these pins and watch your hair tumble to your shoulders." Taking his time, he slowly searched for her hairpins, smoothing each lock into place. "So soft. So silky." He breathed in, tightening his hold, his tone hypnotic. "And scented with spice. Vanilla."

"You're changing the subject."

He nipped her earlobe, then licked away the sting of the tiny love bite. "I have a fondness for sweets."

She trembled at the hunger in his tone, too aware his needs matched her own. She should put a stop to his soft words, quit brushing her pelvis against the denim-covered swell in his jeans.

He nibbled along her neck. "You taste as good as you smell."

"Rand..." This was insane. She had to stop him. But she couldn't. She couldn't think, didn't know what to say. Her thoughts spun crazily as his soft words tugged at her heartstrings.

He nuzzled her neck, his lips inflaming her billowing desire. She shivered again, but from what he'd just said or the wondrous sensation of his fingers combing through her hair while he nibbled and nipped a path down her throat, she wasn't sure. She wasn't sure of anything except that she was exactly where she wanted to be—in his arms.

Kissing him was madness. She trailed her fingers down his shirt, opening buttons and pressing her palms to the warm male flesh, skimmed lower, to his belt.

Rand entwined his fingers in hers, holding her still. "We have to stop."

Her fingers trembled and she jerked back, trying to free her hand. "I...I don't understand." After responding to him gladly, she would have raced out in humiliation at his words, but he held her fast.

"Making love to you now would be taking advantage of the situation."

"What?" He could have taken all the advantage he'd have liked, and her awareness that he knew it sent heat rushing to her cheeks.

"I'm a patient man. I want you to be very sure you want me—that you aren't reacting to the danger."

He must think her a nitwit. With the absence of his touch, except for his hand in hers, sanity returned. Shaking her head to dispel the sensual haze in which he'd wrapped her, she realized that Rand Sinclair was a dangerous man.

Why couldn't she make up her mind? Had his kisses stolen her will? She almost choked on the fact that she'd fully intended to leave Moore House before he'd made her want him. And then he'd withdrawn, leaving her nothing but a bunch of jangled nerves. A basket case of crazy, jittery emotions, a jumble of confusion, reduced to a woman unsure of her own mind.

What game was he playing? Chivalrous Southern gentleman or devious tormentor?

He'd challenged her, taunted her, influenced her with a potent sexual magnetism she'd been unable to resist. Oh, how she wanted him to make love to her. And he'd denied her. She was too confused to think, too aroused to be angry, too frightened by how much she desired him. As he scooped the key off her mother's music box and directed her back upstairs to the attic, she let him lead her. Without one word of protest.

IT WASN'T UNTIL THE KEY clicked in the lock of the attic door that Jasmine's initial curiosity rekindled. Would she find anything about her mother in her father's green chest?

Rand flipped a switch and a bare bulb lit the way. Mold and dust motes rose into the air as she trailed behind, watching her footing on the narrow stairs. If cobwebs existed, Rand's large frame broke through before she reached them.

Despite the lack of scuttling sounds, which would indicate the presence of field mice, rats or squirrels, Jasmine was grateful for Rand's solid presence. When he halted, she almost bumped into him.

"What is it?" she asked, heart thumping.

"I thought Talbot's old chest was at the top of the stairs." Rand rubbed his chin in the dim light, his face cast in dark silhouette by the shadows. "I must have been mistaken."

Jasmine peered around him to where she'd seen the chest earlier. "When Charles left me and I opened the door, I saw the chest right there."

"You're sure?"

Together they climbed the stairs, and she frowned, thinking hard. "I would have bet on it."

Rand squatted, looking carefully at the empty spot on the floor.

"What is it?"

"Look." He gestured. "What do you see?"

"Nothing." Irritation sharpened her tone. Where was all his belief in her? Now even he was questioning whether she was seeing things.

"Look closer."

She leaned over his shoulder and held in a gasp. The faint outline of a rectangle marked the dust, proof the chest had been there. "Someone took it."

"Looks that way." Rand leaned forward. "The edges are smeared, as if someone dragged the trunk toward the stairs. Probably the same person who took the key and placed it in your room.''

He *did* believe her. Despite all the evidence to the contrary, he didn't think she was crazy. She hugged the warm glow of happiness to herself. Right then, her stomach flip-flopped at a sudden realization. Rand Sinclair was a fascinating, dangerous and deceptive man who wouldn't let her go. And she was in love with him.

She'd feared she'd been in trouble before. Now she'd just fallen into the greatest trap of all.

Someone was deliberately impeding her search into the past. But if Rand had moved her father's chest, would he have pointed out the telltale evidence in the dust? If he hadn't been so observant when she'd mentioned that she'd seen the chest, she couldn't have proved her allegation and would seem crazier than an LSD addict on a bad trip.

Well, *this* crazy woman had about all she would take. Rage boosted her courage to fight the madness surrounding her, to confide in the man she loved. ''There's something I haven't told you, something important.''

He stood, one eyebrow arched. ''Yes?''

''Remember the note I found and lost?''

''You've found it?''

She shook her head, mouth dry, wondering how he'd react to her earlier omission. ''The note said my mother is alive.''

In the murky light, she had trouble reading his expression. But at the admission of what he had to see as a betrayal of her confidence in him, a hint of anger entered his tone. ''Why are you telling me now?''

She swallowed past the tightness in her throat. ''I

wanted you to know what I'm hoping to find in this attic.''

''And that is?'' he prompted.

''I've stayed at Moore House not just to search for information about Talbot, but in hopes of discovering where my mother is and if she's still alive.''

''And here I thought *I* might have something to do with your wanting to stay,'' he said lightly.

''I'm sorry for not telling you before.''

He reached out and cupped her chin. ''It's all right. I'm glad you trust me now.''

''Thanks for understanding.'' She pulled away, unable to look him in the eye. She wanted to trust him completely. But somehow she just couldn't. Turning to survey the collection of antiques, junk and memorabilia, she sighed. ''Where should we start?''

''If we're looking for references to your mother, Talbot might have old correspondence in the file cabinets.'' He led her past boxes of old clothing, a radiator, assorted planters and a full set of spoon-backed chairs before stopping in front of file cabinets stuffed with folders.

''I'll start on these,'' he offered. ''Why don't you poke around and see if anything interesting turns up?''

Jasmine had been itching to look in those file cabinets herself, but he appeared so helpful, she'd seem churlish to argue. Besides, she could keep a close watch on him and return later to go through Talbot's old papers herself.

A stack of framed photographs caught her attention. Jasmine flipped through them, recognizing a wedding picture of Irene and Talbot. Irene had been a beautiful woman, more gorgeous for the obvious love for her husband on her radiant face. Jasmine shuffled through the photos but didn't find one of her mother and leaned the stack back where she'd found them.

Searching an old chest of drawers, Jasmine discovered a stack of chemistry books too old for her brothers to have used. "Did Talbot have a chemistry degree?"

Rand looked up. "He was an engineer, a graduate of University of Florida. Why?"

"Just curious who these chemistry books belong to."

"Those were probably Irene's. She used to teach high school chemistry."

At Rand's casual statement, a shudder cascaded down Jasmine's back. Irene had the technical knowledge to start the kind of fire that had killed her father. But Jasmine refused to leap to conclusions, relying on her orderly and practical nature to search for hard evidence.

While she warned herself that she was only beginning her investigation, she searched another drawer of the bureau and found an old journal. Her thoughts raced faster than a computer chip.

Although Rand had scoffed at the idea of Talbot keeping a journal, maybe he'd been mistaken. Almost reverently, Jasmine lifted the heavy book from the drawer. After blowing off the dust, she carefully turned the yellowed pages.

A neat hand had filled in every line of the first page with blue ink. Moving nearer the bare bulb so she could read the meticulous writing, Jasmine took a few minutes to realize the journal was Irene's.

"Rand. Listen to this." She started to read, her

voice trembling with excitement and suspicion. "'Thank the Lord that woman is gone. I love Talbot so much, and he finally feels the same way. He proposed last night. I said yes, yes, yes. He'll never be sorry. Once he's married to me, he'll forget all about her.'"

Chapter Seven

Although Jasmine was eager to question Irene about her diary, the next morning Rand insisted they work on Sinclair and Moore Construction's expense accounts. Since Irene wasn't awake, Jasmine reluctantly agreed.

With Rand taking more than his share of the room, the office seemed smaller than she remembered. Although dressed in baggy jeans and a blue chambray shirt with the sleeves rolled to the elbows, he looked every inch the construction executive and ready to work.

After retrieving the computer file he requested and printing out the expense report, Jasmine stared out the window at the moss-laden oaks, anticipating confronting Irene about her journal and prying information from her. With written proof to back her this time, Jasmine wouldn't accept Irene's lies that she had never heard of Lily Ross.

Jasmine had stayed up half the night reading the journal for any hints that Irene knew what had happened to Lily, but never once had Irene referred to her mother by name. In her heart, however, Jasmine knew Irene had written about her mother, sensed with a frightening certainty that defied logic the comments were about Lily Ross.

Irene's hatred and jealousy had bled through on the yellowed pages as clearly as if the words had been written yesterday. But the sequence and timing of past events eluded Jasmine. Had Irene loved Talbot during the time her mother had been seeing her father? Unfortunately, Irene hadn't dated her entries.

Although Irene certainly had a possible motive for wanting her mother out of the way, Jasmine needed more than suspicions to solve the mystery of her mother's disappearance. She needed facts.

Despite Irene's resentment toward the unnamed woman in Talbot's past, Irene may have had nothing to do with her mother's disappearance. And while Irene might have recognized the significance of Lily's twenty-five-year-old letter, that didn't mean, after two and a half decades had passed, Irene had set fire to the house of her long-departed rival's daughter.

And yet, recalling Irene's chemistry texts in the attic, Jasmine shuddered again at the thought that her mother's rival had advanced technical knowledge about setting fires. Irene could have murdered Talbot.

The fire at Jasmine's house took on new significance. Sticking to her murder scheme by setting fires, Irene might have meant for Jasmine to have been the next victim.

But there was a giant glitch in her thinking. Irene had loved Talbot. Why would she want him dead?

Material details had to be missing, and Jasmine looked forward to asking additional questions, but by lunchtime, Irene and the rest of her family had left the house. Jasmine resigned herself to working through the afternoon and waiting until the dinner hour to ask her questions. Although Talbot's death couldn't have been an accident—not with the fire on his boat and another at his cabin before he'd finally died in the fire at the construction site, she still needed to know who wanted Talbot dead and why before she could connect the pieces of the puzzle.

"Do these figures appear odd to you?" Rand interrupted her concentration on the mystery late in the afternoon and handed her three sheets of paper.

Jasmine perused the long list of expenses, identifying the ones that didn't belong, a car rented over the Fourth of July weekend, flowers, several dinners at expensive Dolphin Beach restaurants and one purchase at a jewelry store for a diamond ring. "These don't look like business expenses, but then I'm unfamiliar with—"

"Keep reading."

She scanned further. "Four cans of gasoline?" Her gaze zoomed in on the date. "The gas was bought two days before my house burned down." Her stomach flooded with acid. She dropped the papers to her lap, her fingers numb, her mind on fast forward.

Rand's eyes hardened. "Your mother's letter was delivered to Moore House, a day later gasoline was bought on the company's account, and then your house burned down. Coincidence?"

Jasmine cautioned herself not to jump to conclusions. "Wait a second. Surely Sinclair and Moore's employees buy gasoline all the time? Don't you have vehicles, trucks and—"

"Underground tanks store gasoline for all company vehicles. We rarely buy gas from a pump. And Blain—"

"Blain?" Her gaze flew to his.

Rand pointed to the identification number at the top of the file. "These are his expense reports, but he wasn't working that day."

"How can you be sure?"

Rand's eyes were bleak. "I authorized a contribution to a volleyball tournament he played in that week."

"Let's see where your idea takes us." Jasmine started a search on her computer. "Maybe we can tie another gas purchase to a date near Talbot's death."

Rand paced while she scrutinized Blain's expense sheets. Judging by the muscle ticking in Rand's cheek, he could barely suppress his rage.

"There's one other gas purchase." She punched up the file. "Here."

"That's exactly one week before Talbot's death." Rand's tone turned grim.

Recalling Blain's youth, she had trouble believing he could have killed his father. "Maybe someone entered the expenses so Blain would *appear* guilty."

"It's possible," Rand conceded, but didn't seem to think her supposition likely.

"Why would Blain want Talbot dead?"

Rand resumed pacing, his thumbs hooked into the waistband of his jeans. "Money."

"I don't understand." Blain liked to lead the life of the idle rich, but he still lived at home. How could he need funds badly enough to murder for them?

Rand's lips tightened as if he wasn't going to say more. But he finally explained. "Blain and Talbot didn't get along. Talbot didn't like Blain's friends, his nonproductive life at the beach, his blatant disregard for working regular hours."

Jasmine watched him pace. "So they argued. Many sons and fathers do."

"The week before his death, Talbot threatened Blain with dismissal from the company if he didn't get his act together."

"What was Blain's response?" Her stomach roiled at the anger beneath Rand's replies. Clearly he didn't like the implications of the gasoline purchases they'd discovered any more than she did.

"Blain laughed in Talbot's face. But that was sheer bravado. Later, he begged me to keep him on the payroll if Talbot followed through on his threat to fire him."

"What did you say?" she asked, interested that Blain had gone to Rand rather than his mother or his Uncle Charles.

Rand swiped a hand through his hair. "Blain put me in a difficult situation, asking me to take sides in a family argument. I needed to think about my answer. One week later, Talbot was dead. Blain's question and my response were moot."

The agony of remorse filled Rand's tone. She stood and went to him, sensing his suspicions about Blain had been eating at him since Talbot's death. Earlier, he'd indicated each of her brothers had his own agenda, but she hadn't guessed Rand actually suspected one of them of murdering Talbot.

The barely leashed regret emanating from Rand wasn't lost on her. His smoldering emotions stirred her compassion.

Moving into Rand's arms was as comfortably familiar as the layout of her computer keyboard. Just as she could type with her eyes closed, she could blindly meld her body to him, snuggle her head under his chin and breathe in his clean scent. Feeling like she'd come home, she cuddled against the steady rise and fall of his broad chest. Despite all her plans—not one of which included loving Rand Sinclair—falling for this man was as delicious and indulgent as licking chocolate off a fresh strawberry.

He reached under her chin and tilted her lips up, his searing gaze mesmerizing. "You're gorgeous." He kissed her with a groan, the touch of his mouth the faintest brush on her lips. "And a distraction."

Wanting more than that first taste of him, wanting to be more than a distraction, she tugged his head down. He kissed her again, spreading his legs wide and encompassing her thighs, his hunger promising to take her where their current problems didn't matter.

His flavor teased her like the Florida sunshine, pure, elemental, hot. His scent brought her a hint of fresh air and male skin. His aura was one of power, striking like lightning, reverberating through her like thunder.

When he pulled away, she felt bereft, as if she were standing in the eye of a raging hurricane, every cell in her body buffeted by the storm that had passed— and braced for more. But as much as she would have welcomed more than his fiercely sweet kiss, now was not the time. He needed answers to the questions that had been haunting him since Talbot's death.

Rand took her hand and squeezed. "Come on. Let's talk to Blain."

"And Irene," she added, quelling the passion flaring inside her. "She has some explaining to do."

IRENE TOOK ONE LOOK at Jasmine and Rand and frowned as if aware something was wrong. Rand paid no attention to Irene's poor-little-me glance, knowing all too well that Charles, who sat opposite Blain at the dining table, would comfort her. As Belle brought in platters of fried chicken, plantains and broccoli with a pitcher of sweet iced tea, Rand pulled out a chair for Jasmine, pleased Blain was home for a change.

Rand had held in his festering suspicions too long. If not for his determination to question Blain about the gasoline purchases, Rand might have been tempted to linger in the upstairs office with Jasmine.

Oh, how she tempted him. Without flirting, without resorting to feminine wiles, she aroused his senses until he ached to explore her sleek, satiny curves. Pride had barely won out over need. He didn't want her coming to him out of fear or obligation. Greedy man that he was, when he took her, he didn't want lies between them.

Although she kissed like an angel, doubts still haunted her eyes. She was the most unpredictable, disconcerting woman he'd ever met. One moment she was determined and defiant, another sensitive and sensuous, the next secretive and teasing.

Positive the secrets he was keeping would come back to haunt him, he wished he was free to confide in her. The necessary lies angered him.

Snapping open his napkin, Rand set it on his lap and turned his focus on Blain. As usual, he looked as if he'd just arisen from a nap. Hair rumpled, unshaven, he had the indolent look of a man deciding whether to return to bed for a snooze or stir himself for a lazy afternoon swim.

Perhaps he'd fooled all of them with his lethargic life-style. Rand picked up his fork. ''Jasmine and I reviewed Sinclair and Moore's expense accounts this afternoon and came across some curious disbursements.''

Irene's lips pursed into a frown. "Really, Rand, it's bad enough T.J. worked late and Art's still downtown. Must you discuss business at the dinner table?''

Beside him, Jasmine left her food untouched and watched Charles, bushy brows raised, pat his sister on the shoulder even as he turned to Rand for answers. "Rand's concerns must be important for him to upset your house rules. What's up?''

Rand had no stomach for the sort of questions he needed to ask, and found his own appetite had vanished. Praying Blain had a reasonable explanation for his expense account, he kept his voice casual. "Blain, tell me about the gas expenditures you made.''

"When?'' Blain asked.

"Shortly before Talbot's death.''

Blain shrugged. "I don't remember.''

"And shortly before Jasmine's house burned down.''

Irene gasped. "Gas expenditures before Talbot's death! Surely you aren't implying that Blain—''

"I'm simply asking why he bought gasoline.'' Rand lowered his voice and kept his tone reasonable and calm.

A twinge of guilt pricked Rand as Irene's face lost color. She dabbed at tears brimming in her eyes. "I don't think—''

"Let the boy answer the question,'' Charles said, backing Rand up and finally losing patience with his sister's constant tears. "I've also noticed the exorbitant expense accounts and had planned to ask Art to justify the charges.''

Rand planted his elbows on the table, leaned forward and pierced Blain with his toughest look. "Well?"

Blain squirmed, refusing to meet Rand's eyes. "I didn't think you'd mind. Especially since you wrote a check to—"

"Why did you buy the gas?" asked Rand, hardening his tone.

Blain looked from Rand to Charles to his mother and licked his lips nervously. "It's not like I was stealing. I do *own* part of the company."

"Yes, you do, dear," Irene said.

Jasmine sat still, practically holding her breath and watching the family proceedings. Rand wondered what she was thinking. Did she regret having come to Moore House to find a family that didn't want much to do with her? Did she see through Irene's practiced tears? Was she horrified that he considered her brother a murder suspect?

Blain slumped in his seat, his voice belligerent. "After the volleyball games, we rent and race Jet Skis. I filled the tanks with gas the week before Dad died and then again last week."

A weight lifted from Rand, a two-ton truckload of dirt removed from a heart compacted with guilt. Blain might be lazy and prefer the beach to the office, but Rand heard the ring of truth in his words. Blain had bought a few gallons of gasoline to race the water vehicles, not to commit murder. The dates of purchase a few days before the fires had been pure coincidence. And there had been no gasoline purchases before Talbot's other close calls with fire.

As if sensing his feelings, Jasmine squeezed his hand beneath the table. Had she guessed how much it hurt him to question Blain so harshly? The more time he spent with her, the more she seemed to know his inner thoughts. A scary notion.

The other purchases, the diamond ring and fancy dinners, paled in importance compared to the gas purchases—so Rand dropped his other questions, deciding to mention those expenses in private. Besides, Jasmine had hard questions of her own to ask, and he could almost feel her gathering her resolve. Apparently she didn't like family squabbles any more than he did.

"Why don't we have coffee in the parlor," Irene suggested.

Once they'd all left the dining table and settled comfortably in the parlor, Rand introduced the new topic for Jasmine.

"We were in the attic last night," he began.

"And found something interesting," Jasmine said hesitantly. There was little Rand could do to protect her from being crushed by her new family's selfish indifference and T.J.'s barely concealed hostility.

From beside the fireplace, T.J. glared at her. "What did *you* find?"

Rand could see her stiffen, but she didn't give in to T.J.'s intimidation tactics. Good. After all she'd been through, Talbot's daughter had the strength and fortitude to find her own answers—and perhaps her own brand of justice.

She pinned Irene with a no-nonsense stare. "I found your journal."

"My what?" Irene covered her mouth, and in the process, knocked over her cup of coffee.

Charles shoved back from the coffee table and shook his head, a resigned expression on his face, as if he'd been expecting Irene's hysterical reaction. The least little thing appeared to set the woman off, and Rand found her tiresome.

At the same moment the coffee cup tipped, Art walked into the room. T.J. took one look at Irene's white, tear-stained face and started shouting at Jasmine to leave before she upset his mother further. Art admonished T.J., trying to make peace, his ears red from embarrassment, while Charles awkwardly attempted to console his sister. Blain ignored everyone.

Jasmine bit her lower lip, looking as if she wanted to crawl under the sofa. Her proud back remained straight and she clenched her fingers at her sides. Clearly she wasn't running from this fight no matter how distasteful she found the family argument, and Rand admired her courage.

"Settle down," Rand shouted. "Art, T.J., take a seat."

Art sheepishly did as Rand asked. T.J. refused and stood behind Irene, literally holding her up. As eldest son, T.J. took his responsibilities seriously. While Rand couldn't fault him for loyalty, life would be easier if he'd lighten up a little and Irene would grow up a lot.

Art relinquished the task of peacemaker to Rand. Blain assumed an amused why-am-I-here expression that used to infuriate Talbot, who often threatened to smack him upside the head. But Talbot had never laid a hand on any of his children. As usual, Charles remained silent, like an outsider unwilling to get involved. In the strained silence, Rand sipped his tea while Belle, eyes downcast, cleaned Irene's spill and left the room.

When he had everyone's attention, Rand spoke in

a quiet tone. "Jasmine and I didn't mean to invade Irene's privacy."

"I want my journal back." Irene pointed to Jasmine. "*You* have no right to read it."

"I already have," Jasmine admitted. "I'm sorry for invading your privacy, but reading your journal wouldn't have been necessary if you'd told me the truth from the beginning."

"What truth?" Art asked, his brow furrowed.

"She told me she hadn't known my mother."

Irene's eyes overflowed with more crocodile tears, and Rand had difficulty restraining his impatience with the woman. Her overreactions were tedious and irritating, and he had to bite his tongue to refrain from snapping at her with impatience.

She grasped T.J.'s hand like a drowning woman holding on to a lifeguard. "I don't have to explain this to her."

"You aren't required to say a word," Charles agreed in a tone he'd use on a fragile witness in court. "But it's understandable that Jasmine is curious about her mother. Once you explain, we can all put this unpleasant business behind us."

T.J. whispered in Irene's ear, too low for Rand to hear. For Jasmine's sake, Rand hoped he'd urge Irene to cooperate.

Belle, her hands shaking, returned to refill the empty coffee cups. The cook and housekeeper had been wrinkled when he was a kid, so she'd always appeared old. Although her spiky orange tufts gave the appearance of energy, she was getting on in years. Rand made a mental note to remind Irene to start training a helper.

"I don't have many memories of my mother," Jasmine spoke softly. "Until I received that lost letter, I'd been told my father was dead." She laced her fingers together in her lap. "You can't imagine my shock upon learning Talbot Moore was my father. I'm curious about my parents, how they met and what happened afterward."

Irene collected herself with a dignity that made Rand positive her tears had been an act. "I don't know much. Talbot and Charles were friends at the University of Florida. Charles occasionally invited me to the Gator football games and introduced me to his friends. I fell in love with Talbot the first time I saw him." Irene sniffled, blew her nose in a tissue. "He was so handsome and strong. But he never noticed me. Charles told me Talbot loved someone else and to forget him—but I couldn't. We were destined for each other. I knew he would love me if he gave me a chance. I was right. We had a good marriage, didn't we?"

Irene asked the question as if she needed reassurance. After all these years, she still seemed unsure of her husband's love. How odd. Rand had never realized how insecure Irene was. Always immaculately groomed, she traveled in elite social circles. He'd never suspected that, all along, she'd been a frightened woman afraid of losing her husband's love—or maybe fearing she'd never had it at all.

"You and Talbot had a fine marriage," Charles reassured her.

"You never met my mother?" Jasmine asked Irene.

Irene shook her head. "I only saw more of Talbot years after your mother disappeared. But my husband never spoke of her—not once. I knew he was thinking about her, of course, and…'' Irene trailed off, as if realizing she shouldn't admit her insecurities out loud.

When she pressed her lips together, undoubtedly done with the conversation, Jasmine turned to face Charles. ''As Talbot's friend, you must have met my mother.''

''Maybe once. I'm not sure.'' Charles took off his glasses and wiped the lenses. ''As I recall, money was a problem. Your mother didn't have transportation and couldn't visit Talbot in Gainesville. He had to stay on campus and study to maintain his grades. I don't think they saw each other often.''

Jasmine frowned and her voice sharpened. ''He saw her often enough to get her pregnant.''

''It takes two, you know,'' T.J. interjected.

Jasmine ignored T.J. and focused on Charles's sympathetic face. ''If you were friends, my father must have mentioned her to you.''

''Once or twice, that's all.''

''He never mentioned me?''

The longing in her tone hit Rand like a punch to the gut. Guilt slithered deep inside, coiling in his throat until he almost choked on his lies. The longer he knew Jasmine, the less he believed she could have been involved in the explosion at the construction site. But until the true culprit was caught, he couldn't trust her completely. Lives were at stake.

Charles removed his glasses again and pinched the bridge of his nose. ''I don't know whether or not Talbot even knew he *had* a daughter.''

Face pale, eyes large and haunted, Jasmine stiffened. ''Then how can you explain Talbot's will? He left his estate to *four* of his children. That indicates he *was* aware of my existence.''

Rand had already had a private discussion with Charles about the will. He didn't want to discuss the legalities now.

Over a sip of coffee, he exchanged a long look with Charles. Jasmine caught the glance and frowned. "What aren't you two telling me?"

Rand had lied enough. He wouldn't tell another.

"You've been so upset about the fire," Charles said. "We didn't want to mention the details before."

"What details?" Jasmine kept her fingers interlocked in her lap, but her eyes glimmered with defiance.

Apparently unperturbed, Charles shrugged. "Before you can inherit assets from Talbot's estate, you'll have to prove your identity."

Irene jumped from the sofa, almost knocking T.J. over. "It's getting late. I feel a migraine coming on and I'm heading to bed. I trust Charles will settle matters to everyone's satisfaction."

Rand expected Jasmine to ask Charles additional questions about the estate. Instead, she, too, rose to her feet. "Excuse me."

After Jasmine hurried down the hall to her room, Rand followed. She met him in the hallway with Irene's journal in her hand. "I'm going to apologize to Irene. T.J. warned me not to upset her, but I didn't realize she was so fragile. I should never have confronted her in front of the family."

Rand suppressed his irritation. Irene's hysterics were the least of his worries. With a possible killer after Jasmine, her safety was paramount—not Talbot's twenty-eight-year-old love affair. "You didn't do anything wrong. And neither did Talbot or Lily.

Irene's hysteria is mostly due to her need for attention."

"Still, she's allowed me to stay in her home. And I repaid her by giving her more grief." Jasmine brushed by him, heading for Irene's room.

Rand increased his pace to keep up with her and arrived as Irene opened the door to the master suite. She hadn't changed the decor since she'd moved into Moore House as a young woman. The room, furnished with a generous sense of family, comfort and taste in the pale colors Talbot had favored, had a lighter, brighter air than the rest of the house.

Irene stood in the doorway. She'd removed her makeup, and her red-rimmed eyes were not a pretty sight.

"I'm sorry to disturb you," Jasmine said, "but I wanted you to have your journal. I shouldn't have intruded on your privacy, but I so wanted to learn about my mother."

Irene grabbed the book and staggered back as if she'd expected to have to fight for it. "You had no right to read this," she said again.

The door opened wider, and Jasmine stiffened with a gasp. Rand leaned forward and directed his gaze to the spot where she stared—at the foot of Irene's chaise lounge.

"Isn't that Talbot's chest?" he asked.

Clutching the journal to her bosom, Irene spun and looked down. "Why, I believe it is. How do you think it got here?"

Jasmine started forward as if drawn to the chest by a magnet. "We were searching for that in the attic."

Irene's eyes narrowed. "Why?"

"I was hoping Talbot might have had a picture of my mother."

Irene tried to shoo them back into the hall with a wave of her hand. But Jasmine planted her feet and placed her fists on her hips, her determination to look inside the chest written all over her lovely face.

"Come back tomorrow," Irene offered wearily. "Right now, I'm going to bed."

"But—"

Rand glanced at his watch and grimaced. He didn't have time to search the chest now. Besides, Irene did look exhausted. If he offered to carry the chest out of her room, she might protest and take back her offer to let Jasmine look tomorrow.

Firmly, he took Jasmine's elbow and tugged. "The morning will be fine. Sleep well, Irene."

As soon as the door closed, Jasmine yanked her arm free, anger shooting like gunfire from her eyes. "Why did you pull me out of there?"

"Irene's possessive about Talbot's things. If you insisted on taking the chest, she might have changed her mind. Besides it's been a long day. We should turn in."

Her doubts and disappointment burned through her stare, scalded his thoughts and incited a riot of guilt. Damn her acute perceptions. Damn him for his lies.

All the while he hurried her down the hall, jiggling the extra key to her room in his hand, knowing if she caught him, she'd hate him for what he'd planned this evening. After searching her room and the private bath to ensure she was alone, he picked up the bed-room key from her bureau and offered it to her.

As she clumsily reached for the key, she knocked it from his hand. The extra key and the original fell onto the floor. Rand scooped both keys up and pressed one into her hand. "I have a spare key. Why don't we lock you into your room?"

Her fingers closed around the key he'd given her. She hesitated, then said, "Okay. I'll probably be safer with the door locked."

The fear on her face had him beating a hasty retreat and steeling himself against her obvious pain. "Don't open this door for anyone but me."

The key clicked in the lock with a finality that left Jasmine confused. Rand left so quickly, she hadn't time to protest. She closed her fingers on the skeleton key Rand had given her until the edges bit into her palm.

How dare he lock the door and walk away without giving her an adequate reason for not searching through Talbot's chest? There was no telling what damage Irene might do in the meantime.

But the chest had been missing since last night. If she wanted, Irene had already had more than enough time to search the contents and remove any evidence that might help Jasmine learn what had happened to her mother. Now that she'd thought over his decision, she realized Rand had been right to leave the chest with Irene. There was no point incurring additional hostility from the woman.

Rand really did have her best interests at heart— even if he was arrogant and high-handed. Although he was only trying to protect her by locking her door, she hated the way he'd taken control, refusing to stay long enough to listen to anything she might have wanted to discuss.

If he hadn't given her the key, she'd be screaming bloody murder right now, using the phone in her room to call for help. No way would she let him keep her a prisoner at Moore House, even if his motive was to protect her.

The walls closed in, and Jasmine ached to throw open the windows and take pleasure in the chirping crickets, croaking frogs and sultry breeze. But the air-conditioning was on, so she turned to her bedside table, idly picked up the telephone receiver and let out a breath of relief at the sound of a dial tone.

She was too suspicious of everyone and calmed herself by remembering Rand's good deeds. He'd offered her a job, a place to stay and had promised to protect her. Several times, he'd taken her side against the family, who owned half his business and had raised him. And he had been wonderful to her. Perhaps she questioned his motives so closely because she didn't trust her growing love for him.

Even now, she longed to go to him. Instead, she placed the key beside her mother's music box and lifted the lid, letting the familiar music soothe her ragged nerves.

Undressing, she drew on a T-shirt over her panties, pulled back the quilt and turned off the light. She snuggled in the sheets, yearning for Rand's male scent and his warm flesh that made her feel safe and cherished. The music slowly died.

Jasmine heard Rand's low murmur. Her eyes flew open and her heart raced. Had he returned? Or had she imagined his voice?

She turned on her light, but no one was in her room. Still, two male voices reverberated through the emptiness, one deep and husky—Rand's—the other a voice she didn't recognize but had heard before. But where?

Tiptoeing to the wall between her room and Rand's, she pressed her ear to the partition. She heard no voices, just footsteps, then silence. Suspicions fully aroused, she forced her mind into high gear. Had Rand hurried her to her room because he had a meeting?

If so, who was he meeting and why had he been so secretive?

Who was in his room at Moore House this late at night? With Rand's room at the rear of the house, conveniently near the back staircase, a secret visitor could easily slip inside without being noticed.

Jasmine debated whether to dress and hide in the stairwell to see who came out of Rand's room.

But Rand hadn't locked her door to keep her in. He unquestionably intended to keep someone out. Should she remain where Rand thought best?

Was he really trying to keep her safe?

Chapter Eight

Hours past midnight, almost at dawn, Jasmine awakened in bed. Low-slung oak branches clawed the roof, clicking like crabs trying to decide on a direction. Groaning, Jasmine rolled to her stomach and snuggled deeper into the covers. She'd tossed and turned for hours past her normal bedtime, thinking about whether she should trust Rand's judgment about leaving her father's chest in Irene's care and who Rand's secret visitor might have been.

Inhaling deeply, Jasmine attempted to relax. A whiff of smoke tickled her nostrils.

No. She must be mistaken.

She sniffed again, and the acrid scent of gasoline fumes and smoke burned her throat, leaving a foul taste in her mouth.

Fire!

Terror skimmed her spine and lodged in her stomach. With a sickening sense of déjà vu, she lunged from bed. Quickly, she dialed 911 and gave the address, and all the while her thoughts whirled. Not another fire. Not again.

Smoke, thick, dark and ugly forced her to take choppy breaths. Without wasting another second, Jasmine grabbed the quilt from her mattress. Covering her shoulders, she barreled through the dark room toward her door. Dense smoke billowed at the windows and clung to the walls, spreading a gloomy pall through the air, impeding her path to the door. Pulse spiking and heart sputtering, she reached for the knob.

Oh, God.

This house had been old twenty-five years old when Talbot had known her mother. After baking for decades under Florida's tropical sunshine, the aged wooden walls would ignite like kindling, blaze into an inferno within minutes. The fire trucks might not arrive in time.

She had to warn everyone. They had to get out. Now.

Twisting the knob, she cursed when the door refused to budge, then remembered Rand had locked her inside. Snatching the skeleton key and her mother's music box, she hurried back to the door, fitted the key into the lock and turned it, waiting for the click to signal her freedom.

The key didn't work.

Her heart jammed in her throat. Someone didn't want her to escape. Had Rand mistakenly taken the wrong key from the rack downstairs and accidently mixed up the two keys when they'd fallen to the floor? Squinting against the smoke that stung her eyes, she pounded the door and screamed.

No one answered. She could barely breathe. In desperation, she set down the music box and clawed at the old-fashioned pins in the door's hinges. Yanking at the rounded tops, she pulled first the bottom pin, then the top pin free.

When the door remained in place, she knelt, shoved

her fingers between the door and the floor and jerked upward with all her strength. Straining, blood roaring in her skull from oxygen deprivation, she dislodged the door from the hinges and toppled it sideways before tumbling into the hall. Behind her, the door fell with a crash loud enough to wake the sleeping Moores and Rand.

Smoke from her room filtered into the hall. Jasmine ran, pounding on doors until the family staggered from their rooms. Clutching the music box in one hand, the quilt in the other, Jasmine stumbled out the front door beside Charles. Rand, wearing slacks but not a shirt was right behind, urging Irene, Art and T.J. to hurry.

"Where's Blain?" Irene shouted, belting a robe around her waist.

Charles helped Jasmine down the front steps. "He's already out here."

Dolphin Bay's neon-yellow fire trucks, sirens screaming, raced to a halt in front of the house. Bleary-eyed, Jasmine lifted her head to spot Blain walking toward them, a gasoline can in his hand. Her muddled thoughts whirled while she focused on Blain, who had bought gasoline the day before her house burned down. Now he'd set Moore House on fire.

Smoke-filled lungs sent her into a coughing fit, but a wild mix of anger, bitter frustration and agonizing fear had her lunging toward her youngest brother. She should have guessed Blain was behind the childish tricks played on her. The mocking laughter she'd heard in her room that day had been his. Blain hadn't been using gasoline for water vehicles at the beach, he'd been using the gas to start fires.

First he'd torched her house, now he'd set Moore House on fire. Thunderous rage clouded her reason and snapped her control. She jabbed her finger in Blain's chest. "You tried to kill me. You set the fire. You're trying to kill us all."

Blain tossed the gas can aside and turned to Rand. "What's wrong with her? Is she crazy?"

Bright, white-hot fury lashed Jasmine into venting a temper she hadn't known existed. That Blain would cast doubt on her sanity after burning her home and business and then attempting murder caused her hysteria to explode. "If you have something to say, say it to my face."

Charles put an arm over her shoulder. "Easy, dear. You're overwrought. Let Rand get to the bottom of this."

Too furious to listen to reason, ignoring the firemen coming up the driveway, Jasmine shrugged from beneath Charles's arm to confront her youngest brother. "Why? Why do you want me dead?"

Blain frowned, his eyes darting nervously right, left, then back over his shoulder. "What the hell is she talking about?"

As if to prevent violence from breaking out, Art moved to stand between Blain and Rand.

Rand crossed his arms over his chest, displaying a calmness that made her want to shake him. "What are you doing with gasoline?"

Blain shrugged. "I was burning fire ants."

"What!" Jasmine couldn't believe he would attempt to talk his way out of arson. They'd caught him with the gas can in his hand!

"It's five o'clock in the morning," Rand said.

"You know I'm a night person." Blain shrugged.

"I've hated the damned ants ever since I first went camping. One of the guys stepped on an ant hill and lost his leg to the bites."

"I don't have fire ants in my room," Jasmine muttered uneasily.

Art pointed to the second story. "But you did leave your window open."

"I knew the air conditioner was on and assumed all the windows would be closed," Blain explained. "If I'd known your window was open, I never would have lit a fire under it."

Taking a good look at the house for the first time, she noted that the building wasn't on fire. All the smoke was coming from the yard.

But she hadn't opened her windows, had she? The room had seemed stuffy. But instead of doing something about it, she'd gone to bed. She was one-hundred-percent sure. Positive. She raised her hand to her throbbing head as the sickening doubts began. Rand had locked the door. No one could have gotten in. Maybe she *had* opened the windows. But why couldn't she remember?

Blain didn't even bother to look up but continued his explanation. "When I noticed the yard was infested, I poured gas on the anthills to set them on fire. But the gas just seeped into the sand and wouldn't burn, so I soaked the Spanish moss with gas to get the fire going. There was no need to call the fire department. I had the hose hooked up. Everything's under control."

Not everything.

Her accusations must have appeared wild. A nauseous feeling cramped Jasmine's stomach. She had accused Blain wrongly. She'd made a total fool of herself in front of the family she'd hoped to become a part of. No doubt about it, her suspicions were way out of control.

But someone was out to kill her. Someone had opened her windows, switched her key. And she had no idea who. Uncertainties had her jumping at every shadow, suspecting simple words and questioning innocent deeds. Damn, but she couldn't recall opening those windows. Maybe Blain was right. Maybe she *was* crazy.

Tears of frustration rolled down her cheeks. She angrily wiped at them, and her hands came away streaked with soot. She was a mess. Her life was a mess. She just couldn't take the pressure anymore. She burst into sobs.

Blain scratched his head and gave her an odd look. "See, I told you she was nuts."

His accusation made her cry all the harder. She tried to speak but couldn't. The more she tried to stop crying, the harder she sobbed. Through the agony of tears, humiliated by the family members' expressions that ranged from pity to discomfort to shock, she clutched the quilt and her mother's music box.

She looked to Rand for support and comfort, but he was walking toward the fireman, leaving Charles to console her.

Jasmine wiped her face with the quilt. "I don't know what's the matter with me."

"It's okay," Charles murmured.

"I never cry…not since…my mother disappeared."

"You've been under a lot of stress. Go ahead and cry."

The Moore brothers made sure the anthill fires

didn't spread. Rand clapped a fireman on the back, no doubt thanking the man and apologizing over her mistake. Finally the trucks drove away. Irene wandered back toward the house, shaking her head and glancing oddly at her.

"Come, Jasmine," Charles said softly. "Let's get you inside."

She shuddered, hating the idea of returning to her room. "C-could I wait for Rand on the porch?"

"Of course, whatever will make you feel better." Charles guided her up the steps and seated her in a rocker before tucking the quilt around her.

She wondered if he was always this nice. Or perhaps he was just going out of his way so she'd cast her suspicions elsewhere. Oh, God, she was doing it again. An old man couldn't be nice without her paranoia setting in.

"You need to relax. Perhaps learn some simple breathing techniques. I could arrange for you to talk to a psychiatrist who could teach you."

Rand took the steps two at a time. "I think she should talk to Dylan. I'd like his professional opinion."

"Dylan?" Jasmine asked.

Rand took the seat beside her and entwined his fingers with hers. "Dylan Wade's a friend of mine."

"You think I need to talk to a psychiatrist?" Her stomach sank at the realization Rand had lost faith in her judgment.

"Dylan's a cop." Rand squeezed her hand, his thumb rubbing soothing circles over her wrist. "If confirming your sanity by talking to a shrink will make you feel better, go ahead. But don't do it for my sake. I have no doubts about you."

Rand's loyalty chased away the morning chill. Her friendship with him had kindled into a fiery love. His understanding, confidence and forgiving meant the world to her.

He hadn't once castigated her for her disturbing everyone's sleep or even calling the fire department for a false alarm. The thought banished the last of her doubts. His actions had just proved he would give her his loyalty through good times and bad.

How could she not love him? She cherished his unwavering support, adored his loyalty. If the problems at Moore House didn't faze his steadfast belief in her, neither would the minor irritations of day-to-day living, small disappointments or the compromises necessary to make a relationship grow.

Squeezing his hand, she wished she never had to let go. Her love for him had made up for the loss of her home and business. If she didn't have his love in her life, no matter what else she had, it would never be enough. But did he reciprocate her feelings?

AFTER BREAKFAST, RAND retrieved Talbot's chest from Irene's room. "I took a peek and the contents are dusty. Better to make a mess out on the porch and not add to Belle's work."

Jasmine followed him, appreciative his concern for others included the hired help. "I've spent too much time inside recently. Maybe the fresh air will clear my head."

A respite from the rest of the family was welcome. T.J.'s festering anger as he glared across the breakfast table, Irene's embarrassment over Jasmine's mistake, Art's forced cheerfulness, Blain's laid-back amusement and Charles's determined effort to ignore the entire incident had all begun to wear on her nerves. Only Rand believed in her, and she tried to put her overreaction to the fire behind her.

Despite mysteriously opened doors, missing keys and a false fire alarm, she was finally going to search Talbot's chest. She opened the front door wide and Rand carried the box into the dappled sunlight before setting it down.

He dragged over a chair for her, then flipped open the lid. "Don't expect too much."

T.J. marched onto the porch. "She's been expecting too much since she got here."

Rand dusted his hands and stood, leaving the chest's contents to her. "And you haven't said one friendly word to your *sister* since she arrived. Your attitude could use an adjustment."

Jasmine wasn't up to arguing. Gingerly she picked up a moldy green army jacket and set it aside, grateful for Rand's defense, leaving her free to explore the rest of the box.

"My *attitude* isn't the problem," T.J. countered. "She is."

"Really?" Rand drawled.

"Don't give me your superior attitude. Ever since she's arrived, Mother has been depressed."

"Irene's in mourning. She was depressed before Jasmine arrived."

"Jasmine is making things worse. She's stirring up the past. Digging into things that don't concern her."

"Can it." Rand scowled and lowered his voice to a menacing level. "Jasmine has every right to ask questions about her father. Why can't you understand? While you were growing up in the lap of luxury and surrounded by love, she grew up without a father or a mother."

Rand understood her so well. Too well. Her heart ached for the lonely children they had both been.

Flinging aside several moth-eaten sweaters and two pairs of denim jeans, Jasmine feared the chest was another dead end. But a breeze picked up, the overhead branches swayed and sunlight glinted off a piece of metal. Stashed in the chest's bottom corner was a piece of jewelry. Two pieces of blackened silver.

Earrings. Dangling silver earrings with bells.

Her stomach did a double flip. She clutched them close to her chest, her heart lifting with joy. Talbot wouldn't have saved these earrings if Lily Ross hadn't meant something to him. "These were my mother's."

"Can I see?" Rand held his hand palm up.

Reluctant to give them up, she stood and held the earrings by the clasps.

T.J. glared at her with suspicion. "You sure they were your mother's?"

"Positive. She was wearing them in my favorite picture of her." She shook the bells gently and smiled at the soft tinkle. "I always wondered if the bells rang."

Rand's hand enclosed hers around the earrings. His eyes softened at her pleasure. "Now you know."

T.J. shattered the moment. "Do you have this picture?"

"It burned in the fire with the rest of my things."

"As usual, you have no proof. You expect us to take your word."

Jasmine knew Rand would continue to support her,

but she'd had enough of T.J.'s nastiness. "We could ask Irene if they're hers."

T.J. spun on his heel and left without another word.

Rand grinned. "Remind me never to argue with you."

"Why?" she asked, with as innocent a look as she could manage.

"Because you deliver a knockout punch with so little effort."

"I was bluffing. I'd never deliberately cause Irene pain."

"You're probably a hell of a poker player." His eyes turned smoky as he teased her. "I'll have to remember how dangerous you really are."

She cocked her head at a saucy angle. "You better watch out, mister." And then she tugged him toward her, and instigated what she hoped was a playfully sexy embrace.

Crushing her to him, Rand didn't disappoint her. A delicious shudder heated her. Drugged by his clean scent, captivated by his strength, dazzled by his ability to understand what she wanted before she said the words, she lost herself in a long, wonderful kiss.

RAND ONLY FOUND the strength to break away from Jasmine's kiss when someone cleared his throat and chuckled. That she had so enchanted Rand that he hadn't heard Dylan park his green-and-white police cruiser in the driveway said more than he wanted to admit about how much he cared for Jasmine Ross.

She reeked of smoke, dirt smudged her chin and her eyes were still red from her former tears, but she was the most beautiful woman inside and out that he'd ever known. As passion receded and she noticed Dylan, her face turned a lovely shade of crimson.

Women usually fawned over his friend, who was tall, classically handsome, with light brown hair and warm eyes. Although Rand kidded the policeman that he had the advantage of a uniform to attract women, Mother Nature had blessed Dylan with good looks. Dylan greeted them with a lazy nod.

Rand took Jasmine's hand. "I'd like you to meet a friend of mine. As a favor to me, he's promised to help you out. Dylan works for the Dolphin Bay Police. Although the fire at your home in Seffner is out of his jurisdiction, I've asked him to make unofficial inquires for us."

"Any help would be appreciated." Jasmine was polite. "Would you two rather I leave when you're conducting business?"

"I'm always glad to—"

"Why do you ask?" Rand interrupted Dylan and turned to her.

She shrugged but eyed Rand with a perceptive stare. "Last night I heard you talking to a man in your room. I got the idea you didn't want me around."

Rand kept his voice casual and hoped neither Jasmine nor Dylan would pursue the matter. "Must have been the radio." He steered Jasmine to a seat on the porch, sat beside her and gestured for Dylan to do the same. "Have you found anything interesting?"

"More than interesting." Dylan's lips turned up in a pleased expression. "I think I've found a connection between the fire that killed Talbot and the arsonist who torched Jasmine's house."

Jasmine's fingers twisted in her lap. "You have

proof the same person that killed my father is after me?''

''Not exactly proof.'' Dylan opened a briefcase stuffed with official-looking documents. ''Let me start with the facts. The state crime lab analyzed chipped concrete samples from the construction site where Talbot died. Gasoline was used as an accelerant, ignited when the acetylene tank exploded.''

Jasmine frowned. ''What does that mean?''

''From the evidence in this report, it appears the murderer released gas into an enclosed area. Any spark would cause an explosion.''

Rand nodded. ''And gasoline was used to fan the fire.''

''Exactly.''

Jasmine looked from Rand to Dylan. ''I don't see what that has to do with the fire at my house.''

Dylan held up a finger. ''I'll get to your house in a minute. I want to back up a bit first.''

''To the other attempts on Talbot's life?'' Rand guessed, confirming the suspicions he'd been harboring by the grim set of Dylan's jaw.

Dylan pulled out another paper. ''The fire on Talbot's fishing boat was caused by a gas leak. Anyone could have sliced the line.''

''But?'' Rand pressed him.

''The fire at the hunting cabin was a little more sophisticated. Our perpetrator spilled gasoline around the doors and windows. In addition, the arson investigator found an empty but *intact* tank of liquid propane gas lying on the ground.''

''I don't understand,'' Jasmine said.

''This is where the supposition part comes in,'' Dylan explained. "I think the arsonist considered using the gas in the tank of Talbot's grill to start the fire."

"But the tank was empty?" Rand guessed again.

Dylan nodded. "He may have bought a new tank that had never been filled."

Jasmine turned to him, questions in her eyes. "How could you know the tank was empty?"

Rand took her hand. "Because it was still intact."

"So if there was gas inside, the tank would have exploded," Jasmine said, following his reasoning. "But you can't be sure the arsonist planned to use the tank. Besides, what difference does it make if he did?"

The frustration in her voice tugged at Rand. He wished he could solve the problem for her, or at least level with her. Soon, he promised himself, the lies would be behind them.

"Did you have a gas grill at your house?" Dylan asked Jasmine.

She shook her head.

"Not everything burns in a fire," Dylan explained. "Carpet samples from the ashes of your house were also sent to the crime lab. Again, gasoline was the accelerant."

"But that doesn't prove anything," Jasmine protested.

Rand put an arm over her shoulder and murmured into her ear. "Patience."

Dylan reached into his briefcase and pulled out another stack of papers. "But the Seffner arson investigator found pieces of a liquid propane tank in the ashes of your home."

But Jasmine had just said they didn't have a grill.

Was Dylan suggesting that the arsonist had brought the tank of gas with him?

Jasmine stiffened. "I did hear a loud noise, like a rifle shot, shortly before I discovered the house was on fire. I thought a car engine had backfired."

"More likely you heard the tank explode."

"Then why am I still alive?"

"You were lucky. According to this report, the refrigerator blocked most of the blast."

Rand rubbed her shoulder, wishing he could pull her onto his lap. "But even a small explosion was enough to ignite the gasoline and start the fire."

"Exactly." Dylan tossed the papers onto the chair beside him. "My point is that if Jasmine didn't have a propane tank, the arsonist probably brought it with him."

"He used the same tactic in the fire that killed Talbot?" Rand asked.

"Sort of. This arsonist is not a professional. The attempts are clumsy. But each fire is more deadly. Each trap more refined."

"I suppose police protection for me is out of the question?" Jasmine asked.

"I'm sorry. We don't have the manpower for twenty-four-hour surveillance."

"Why does whoever killed my father also want me dead? What's the motive?"

Rand didn't have to think twice. "Money."

"Talbot's estate." Dylan nodded. "That makes sense. Who stands to gain the most from Jasmine's death?"

"Me. Because I'd gain control of the company."

"Who else?" Dylan asked.

"Everyone in this family likes money. T.J. likes to

control it. Art likes to count it. And Blain likes to spend it.''

"What about Irene?'' Dylan asked.

Rand shook his head. "Talbot set up a trust for her. She has nothing to gain from murder.''

"Except more money for her sons,'' Dylan said.

Jasmine sighed, obviously discouraged. Rand couldn't imagine what it was like to finally find her family, then be forced to consider one of them was determined to kill her. Still, she didn't duck the hard questions.

"Does Charles own any stock?'' she asked.

Rand shook his head.

"What about Belle?'' Jasmine inquired. "Does she get anything?''

Rand had thought he'd turned over every possibility, but he hadn't ever considered Belle might have a motive. "She receives a minor bequest. Why?''

"I don't know,'' Jasmine said. "I just have this feeling she knows more than she's saying.''

Rand turned back to Dylan, wondering how they could use what they'd learned. "What do you recommend?''

Dylan's brown eyes looked at Jasmine as he answered the question. "The way I see it, she has two choices. One, she can run and hide.''

"And spend the rest of my life looking over my shoulder?'' Jasmine shook her head. "No, thank you. That's no way to live.''

"Or you stay close to Rand, hope the arsonist tries again and that we'll catch him before he gets you. If the arsonist is a family member, you're probably safest here at the house. Unless whoever it is wants to eliminate all the legal heirs but himself.''

"What are the chances of catching this guy?" Jasmine asked.

Dylan grimaced. "On the basis of what we know now, not good. In the meantime, stay close to Rand. The closer, the better. If fact, don't let him out of your sight."

JASMINE INSISTED ON returning to the attic after Dylan had left. She'd appeared to have put memories of Blain's fire behind her and had taken Dylan's warning better than Rand expected. Although she'd broken down after the fire at Moore House, there was a core of strength in Jasmine Ross that reminded him of Talbot. She had the same courage, the same innate manners, the same stubbornness to succeed. Rand couldn't help wondering what making love to a woman with such a strong passion for life would be like. He imagined she'd be his equal without losing one iota of femininity.

Jasmine held up her mother's jewelry. "Now that I know Talbot saved these earrings, I'll bet there's a picture of her around somewhere."

Rand supposed fixating on finding a picture was better for her than dwelling on a killer coming after her. Although he'd prefer to go through the expense reports now to look for purchases of liquid propane gas tanks, the reports could wait.

With the stress she'd been under, it was a wonder Jasmine could think rationally. If searching for clues to her mother's disappearance made her happy, he was glad to accommodate her.

As he helped her move a large picture frame blocking an old desk, Rand debated how to broach the topic of her safety. He couldn't protect her at night from another room. Different sleeping arrangements had become a necessity.

Unable to think of a casual way to introduce the topic, he spit out his thoughts. "I think we should sleep together."

"Excuse me?" Eyes wide with surprise, Jasmine turned around to look at him and knocked over a stack of books.

He strode closer to her. At least he had her full attention and he rather liked it. "I didn't say that right. Dylan said not to let you out of my sight. I intend to take him at his word."

She fisted her hands on her hips, a smile playing lightly over her lips. "So what are you saying?"

"I'm sleeping in your room tonight."

"Where?" She didn't sound outraged. In fact, she sounded as if she was trying not to break into song. Her easy tone had him pulsating with a need that would soon be evident if she didn't curb the blatant desire in her eyes.

"Where would you like me to sleep?" he countered.

"Do I have to do all your thinking for you?"

God, he enjoyed seeing this light side of her, the smile on her lips, a sassy light in her eyes. He had nothing but admiration and desire for the strong will she must have exerted to put aside her other problems.

He cocked an eyebrow. "You don't have any objections?"

"Not if you sleep in my bed." She spoke with a boldness that appeared to surprise her. Her face flushed.

"It's a very small bed."

But she didn't back down. "And you're a large

man. I imagine I'll bump into you occasionally. Are you sure you won't mind?"

Mind? The thought had him teetering on a dangerous precipice between frustration and anticipation, as eager as a senior on prom night. And less prepared. He made a note to make a trip to the local pharmacy before bedtime.

Jasmine stepped toward him, over the books, the mischievous light in her eyes welcoming him. She opened her mouth to say something. And tripped.

He reached to catch her and they tumbled, laughing, onto the attic floor in a jumble of arms and legs. Something jabbed him in the back. He pulled a clipboard out from under him, started to toss it aside. Her hand on his wrist stopped him.

"Wait." Jasmine took the clipboard. Pulling out a piece of paper trapped beneath the clip, she gasped, and the smile died on her lips. Her face paled. "Someone must have torn off the paper without realizing they'd left the letterhead beneath."

"What is it?" From his angle, he couldn't see the paper, but when she'd stiffened, he guessed she'd found something significant.

"It's the top of a piece of business stationery." Her voice trembled with excitement or anger, he wasn't sure which. "A form. Or an invoice." Her hands shook. "From Bayside Hospital."

"Bayside? That's a small, private psychiatric hospital just a few miles from here."

"A mental institution?"

"Mostly a retreat for the very wealthy who're having trouble coping with their lives. But no one in this family was ever admitted there. So what's the invoice doing here?''

"Look.''

In the top right corner a name had been scrawled in neat handwriting. Lily.

Chapter Nine

"Don't get your hopes up," Rand warned Jasmine, worry flickering across his concerned face. "That paper looks old. Even if the Lily mentioned is your mother, a lot could have happened since that was written."

Jasmine so badly wanted to find her mother, she barely listened. Could Lily Ross have entered Bayside Hospital all those years ago? Was that why she'd never come home from an afternoon errand?

A myriad of thoughts flashed through Jasmine's mind, swirling like cosmic dust. Her mother might have had an accident, a head injury. She could be in a coma. Or like her daughter, she could have begun to see and hear things. The sudden awareness of the possibility of mental illness running in her family had Jasmine focusing differently on the past few days.

Before she could discuss her horrible misgivings with Rand, Charles called from the third floor. "Rand? I need to talk with you."

Rand took her elbow, helped her up from the floor. "Give us a second." Quickly they restacked the pile of books she'd tripped over and came down the stairs.

"I'm glad I found you." Charles mopped his brow

with a handkerchief. "One of our loaders backed into Joe Blackwell's truck, injuring him."

"How badly is he hurt?" Rand asked.

"He could lose his arm. He's at Dolphin Bay Memorial Hospital."

"I'll go over there and make sure he receives the best care. Have someone pick up his wife and bring her to the hospital."

"I'll come with you," Jasmine offered. Belle had been right about how much Rand cared for his employees. Concern was written all over his face.

Charles glanced at his watch, then at Jasmine. "Oh, I almost forgot. Dr. Mason called back and agreed to see you this afternoon as a favor to Rand."

"Dr. Mason?"

"A psychiatrist." Rand encompassed both her hands in his. "I called him this morning, after the fire when you were so upset."

Hysterical would have been more accurate, but her first reaction to the appointment was annoyance. If she wanted to see a shrink, she could make her own arrangements.

And probably wait weeks for an appointment, her conscience argued.

Charles stuffed the handkerchief into his pocket and glanced at his watch again. "I've been worried about you, too, Jasmine. We could drop you at Dr. Mason's on our way to the hospital. His office is near there, and you can call Rand to pick you up after you're done."

She'd always hated doctors. Probably because every time she had consulted one, never for anything serious, he never seemed sure of a diagnosis. However, after suspecting that her mother might have been institutionalized, she had some questions about inheriting mental instabilities and she wanted an objective viewpoint on her strange experiences. Perhaps talking to Dr. Mason was a good idea.

"Thanks. Let me change into something suitable."

Charles insisted Jasmine take the front seat while he rode in the back of Rand's car. The men spoke about insurance, a safety investigation and the injured driver's excellent work history and driving record, and Jasmine's thoughts returned to the attic.

Although she was excited at finding the partial letterhead bearing Lily's name, she put aside the thoughts of finding her mother. She needed to decide how to present to Dr. Mason in a logical manner the unusual things that had happened to her.

Concentrating proved impossible. Instead, she slipped back to the moment when Rand had told her he intended to sleep with her tonight. She had no idea what had come over her, but she'd never felt more feminine, more desirable in her life. She'd become— not someone else—but more free to be herself. At hearing he wanted her, all the inhibitions she'd been repressing had vanished.

Either somewhere inside her was a bold, passionate woman or the mental aberrations she'd experienced were now also affecting her personality. Had Rand torn down walls to liberate her, or was she undergoing another symptom of mental instability? Uncertain, nevertheless Jasmine decided she liked this new brazen and reckless person.

In other relationships, she'd stood back, observing, planning, careful not to lose control, her emotions established within self-imposed boundaries. But with Rand, her restrictions disappeared, leaving her unfettered by prudish constraints. She liked the swept-away feeling, the giddy excitement when she was with him.

All her life she'd been so careful not to grow too attached, fearful that whomever she loved would leave her like her parents had. But Rand had seen her at her worst. He'd seen her fall apart. And he still wanted her. His support gave her the confidence to commit her heart.

A few days ago, she would have been devastated to learn her mother might have been sent to a mental facility. Today, she could face anything because Rand had said he wanted her. She'd seen the desire darken his bedroom eyes, heard the husky promise in his voice, felt the heat of his passion pressed against her.

Although he hadn't yet said he loved her, what he *had* said was enough to keep her hopes soaring. Optimistic that everything would turn out fine, she waved good-bye to Rand and Charles and entered Dr. Mason's office. She'd never been as happy in her life. She couldn't be losing her mind.

But she fully expected Dr. Mason would confirm she was crazy.

Crazy in love.

JASMINE AND RAND walked through a park near the hospital where Charles remained, spelling Rand from his vigil. Joe Blackwell was still in surgery. Charles had promised to call Rand on the cell phone if there was any news.

After they bought cold drinks, Rand led her to a bench shaded by an oak tree. "You needn't tell me what Dr. Mason said if it makes you uncomfortable."

She sipped her cola, pleased he wasn't demanding,

but asking, to hear Dr. Mason's diagnosis. Rand possessed an innate politeness that stemmed from his confident nature. Almost as if he'd made his decision about her, giving her a thumbs-up, and fully expected Dr. Mason to confirm his opinion.

"Actually, talking to Dr. Mason was interesting. He began by taking my history. We both thought it significant that no unexplainable events happened before my house burned down."

Rand gazed at her with eyes that reflected his confidence in her. "I'm not surprised."

At the warm admiration in his expression, Jasmine suddenly imagined a lifetime of basking in his approval. She imagined the two of them together in this park forty or fifty years from now. Rand's eyes would be just as gray and compassionate, his shoulders just as broad. And she'd love him every bit as much as she loved him right now.

Loving him made sharing the rest of what Dr. Mason had said easier. "He mentioned post-traumatic stress syndrome can cause concentration loss and forgetfulness, and can affect clarity of thinking. He offered me drugs."

Rand frowned. "What did he prescribe?"

"I refused to take anything. I was afraid taking them would make me more confused." She risked another look at his eyes but saw nothing but approval.

"There's nothing wrong with your thinking."

"You'll be happy that Dr. Mason agreed with you—mostly."

"Mostly?"

"Well, he didn't come right out and make a diagnosis. Shrinks don't work that way. Mental illness isn't black and white. There are many stages of gray between.''

"So the good doctor wouldn't commit himself for fear of making a mistake?" Rand's tone expressed a cynical disdain.

"That's possible. But he did ask what I thought about the incidents I couldn't explain, like hearing voices in your room.'' Or how easily she'd fallen in love with him. She thought Rand flinched, but then realized she must have been mistaken when he faced her squarely. "We discussed why someone might play tricks on me, that kind of thing.''

Anger filtered through Rand's concern. "Burning down your house is more than a trick.''

"Agreed." Jasmine sighed, weary from forging rational explanations for the unexplainable. "But the warning note's disappearance, the missing key, the chest in the attic showing up in Irene's room, and the open windows in my bedroom can't be easily explained away.''

"So what did Dr. Mason think?" Rand asked. How could he remain so calm when they had such few answers?

Perhaps her tension didn't stem from a lack of answers. Rand sat so close to her, even without his touch, she was enveloped by his warmth. He looked so good in a white chambray shirt, gray slacks and sports coat that heat curled in her stomach.

Thinking about the conversation in Dr. Mason's office was hard when Rand's promise to stay with her tonight was a priority in her mind. But she made an effort to suppress the sudden desire to kiss him again. "Dr. Mason asked a lot of questions and made some suggestions.''

"Like what?"

"He showed me breathing exercises. And muscle relaxation, where I concentrate on loosening each part of the body, one at a time." The thought of being able to loosen her muscles was ridiculous. Right now she felt stretched tighter than a taut wire.

Rand's voice rose in skepticism. "That's it?"

No. She wanted him to tell him how much she was looking forward to tonight—but she didn't quite dare. And that wasn't what he was asking, anyway.

Drawing her wandering thoughts to a stop, she forced herself to remember Dr. Mason's instruction. "To help concentrate, I'm supposed to take stock of my life, write lists and pick a task to accomplish each day."

"And?"

"I'm a very organized person." Succumbing to her deepest musings, she let the smile inside spread to her mouth. Damn it. There was nothing wrong with showing him how much she wanted him. "I've already picked what I want to do today."

Rand's eyebrow arched, signaling he'd caught her innuendo. "Can I be of service?"

Jasmine chuckled happily, feeling the boldness frothing and bubbling inside her, eager to come out. Had she finally succumbed to the stress by casting aside all inhibitions? She didn't know. But she could no longer hold back the impudent woman inside. "What I have in mind cannot be done without you."

"Tell me more."

After numerous hot kisses that had left her frustrated, she thought it only fair to give him a spicy taste of his own passion-fermenting potion. Tonight was going to be special, and she wanted him to look forward to it as much as she was. "It's been a long, hot day. I thought we'd shower together."

His marvelous eyes widened, twinkling with pleasure and surprise. "A shower?"

"To cool off."

He swore under his breath. "If you think taking a shower with you will cool me off—"

"I've always had trouble reaching my back. Between my shoulder blades." She bit her lip to hold back her amusement. As she hoped, Rand drew a ragged breath, appearing incapable of taking his eyes off her mouth. With a naughty grin, she licked her lip. She'd never known teasing a man could be so enjoyable and empowering. What was the matter with her? Was she in love or was she crazy? And how could she tell the difference?

Rand groaned.

"I like warm showers—not too hot, not too cold. First I tip my face up to the spray, let the drops trickle through my hair and over my shoulders and…well, you get the idea."

"Yeah, I get the idea," he rasped. "Do you have any idea what you're doing to me?"

She ignored his question, glad that just a few words could disconcert him as much as just sitting beside him affected her. "I like to be wet all over before using the soap. Just thinking about your hands on my slick, bare back warms me."

"Jasmine—"

"You will help me, won't you?"

"With your back?"

"Wherever you want."

"I don't think—"

"Of course, if you don't like showers, we could take a bath."

He sucked in his breath.

"In the whirlpool tub out on the back patio. We'd wait until everyone is asleep. We'd undress each other in the moonlight. Imagine the night breeze on bare, wet skin. Bubbling, warm water. Birds cooing. Raspberry liquid soap." She lowered her voice to a husky murmur. "And I picture you beside me, caressing—"

"Enough, woman!" Rand pulled her against him, kissing her as if he couldn't get enough. "Don't say another word unless you're ready for me right this instant."

She *was* ready for him, here on the park bench in front of everyone.

Surely, she'd lost her mind.

"YOU WANT TO GO WHERE?" Art asked Jasmine.

Positive Rand would spend the rest of the afternoon at the hospital, but hopefully thinking of her after the images she'd planted in his mind, Jasmine sat beside Art in his car.

Although Jasmine hadn't discussed the side trip with Rand, she had the afternoon free to look for her mother while he stayed at the hospital. With Art driving, she felt safe enough to search Dolphin Bay's only private psychiatric facility.

"Take me to Bayside Hospital," she requested calmly.

Art speared her with a suspicious glance, but his tone remained pleasant. "That shrink didn't talk you into committing yourself, did he?"

"I'm going there to look for my mother." Jasmine

told Art about the paper she and Rand had found in the attic, and he listened attentively.

"Does Rand know about this?"

"I thought he had enough on his mind without worrying over me. Besides, if you stay with me, Rand won't mind."

Art ran a hand through his dark hair. "I don't like hospitals."

"Does anyone?" Jasmine shuddered at the prospect of finding her mother at Bayside. If she was there, what state of mind would she be in?

"I know it sounds silly," Art said, interrupting her thoughts, "but ever since I had my appendix out as a kid, I've dreaded hospitals. The antiseptic smell brings back bad memories and nightmares."

Jasmine reassured him, worried Art might take his guard duty too seriously and she might not get to search for her mother. "You needn't come inside with me. Surrounded by people, I'm sure I'll be safe in a hospital. You could wait in reception or in the car. After all these years, I can't imagine my mother will still be here. But I have to look."

"We could call."

"Please. I've looked up the address—it's not far. I've wondered all my life what happened to her. She walked out one day and never came back. I'd like to know the truth."

"All right." Art shrugged. "You've convinced me. After I drop you off, I'll read the paper in the car and catch up on the stock market."

"I might be a while. The records I need them to check are twenty-five years old."

THE RECEPTIONIST SCOWLED when Jasmine mentioned 1972, the year her mother had disappeared.

The streaked-blond-haired woman behind the desk snapped her chewing gum and pointed with her pencil to a monitor. ''We computerized five years ago. There's not much call for records that old, but the administrator might be able to help you if you want to hang around.''

Jasmine didn't want to ask Art to wait longer than necessary. ''Could you see if there's a patient here by the name of Lily Ross?''

''I told you, I don't have the old records.''

''But if she's still here, she'd be in the computer, wouldn't she?'' Jasmine argued between gritted teeth. A man ambled by, a baseball cap hiding his features, and she assumed he was a patient.

''What's the name again?''

''Lily Ross. R-O-S-S.''

The receptionist typed the name on her keyboard and stared at her monitor. ''There's no one here by that name.''

''Are you sure?'' Unwilling to accept defeat, Jasmine persisted. ''Maybe you spelled her name wrong?''

''There is no Lily Ross here, ma'am. See for yourself.'' The woman swung the screen around in disgust.

A glance told Jasmine she'd once again raised her hopes for nothing. ''Thanks, anyway.'' She'd have to return at another time and speak to the administrator to follow up on the old records.

Disappointment slowed her steps as she headed toward the front door. A young woman with gaunt cheekbones, sunken eyes and a belted bathrobe tied much too tight shuffled over to Jasmine in bedroom slippers. "Looking for Lily?"

Jasmine looked at the patient warily, thinking she appeared as sane as the next person. "Yes?"

"I know Lily."

"Lily Ross?"

"Lily." The woman slipped her hand into Jasmine's. "Come. I'll show you Lily."

Jasmine began to doubt the wisdom of accompanying the woman. Looking more closely, she noted the dilated pupils that indicated she was medicated. But the patient seemed so certain she knew Lily that Jasmine couldn't bear to go back to Moore House without checking.

Although Jasmine supposed she might be breaking visiting rules, no one stopped their progress. Hoping the violent patients were in locked wards, she let the woman lead her to a private room off the main corridor.

After releasing her hand and giving her a gentle shove toward an open door, her guide walked away, saying, "Lily is a good woman. A good woman."

Jasmine hesitated, inhaled a deep breath and let the air out slowly, using one of the relaxation techniques Dr. Mason had taught her. But no relaxation technique could cure twenty-plus years of burning curiosity over her mother's disappearance.

Rapping her knuckles lightly on the open door, tagged with the name Lily Smith, Jasmine called out, "Lily."

When no one answered, she ignored her clammy hands and entered the dim room. Light filtered in through closed blinds. A woman sat in an easy chair. Her head was capped with short silver hair that needed a good brushing. In silhouette, her facial features were indistinct. Her thin arms crossed over her as she rocked back and forth, oblivious to Jasmine's presence.

At the pitiful sight, nausea rose in Jasmine's stomach. This woman couldn't be the kind, beautiful woman who smelled so good, whose loving touch she remembered. This woman was too small, too out of it. No, she couldn't be her mother.

"I'm sorry, I was looking for Lily."

The woman continued to rock. She didn't say a word. But she started to hum a tune so familiar, the notes rooted Jasmine's feet to the floor. She knew that tune. She listened to it every night after she wound her mother's music box.

A lump of horror, fear and happiness swelled her throat tight. She might not recognize her mother from twenty-five-year-old pictures, so how could she identify Lily Ross? Although her profile resembled Jasmine's memories of old photos in Aunt Daisy's album, she couldn't be sure this woman was her mother.

Oh, God! What should she say? Where should she begin? Coming here had seemed so simple after she was buoyed up by her lunch with Rand. She hadn't planned what to say, how to begin.

Turning to Lily, Jasmine took a seat beside her. She had so many questions. Ones that might never be answered. But for the moment, it was enough to sit beside Lily and gently take her hand. The woman's hand was exactly the same size and shape as Jasmine's, with long fingers and gently curved nails.

Lily yanked her hand back. She stopped humming. "Do I know you?"

That the woman had spoken was wonderful, but if she was Jasmine's mother, would she even remember the daughter she'd left so long ago?

"Do I remind you of someone?" Jasmine asked, her heart pounding with hope.

Lily stared at her for a long minute. "Maybe, Sweet Flower. Maybe not."

Oh, God! Sweet Flower had been her mother's nickname for Jasmine when she'd been a little girl. Between the tune she'd hummed that matched the music box, her dearly remembered profile and the nickname, Jasmine was convinced. She'd found her mother.

Swallowing the lump of happiness in her throat, Jasmine couldn't believe her good luck. After all the years of wondering, she finally had a mother and part of the answer to the question that had haunted her for so long. But how her mother had come to be here still remained a mystery.

"Do you remember Talbot Moore?" Jasmine asked.

Lily's eyes filled with tears that overflowed onto her cheeks. Eerily, she cried without making a sound.

At a loss to know what to do or say, Jasmine awkwardly patted her mother's shoulder. During the passing years, their positions had reversed. Now Lily was the one who needed her daughter's help.

And God help her, Jasmine didn't know if she was up to a conversation. Suppose she said something that set her mother off again? Suppose she became violent?

How long since her mother had been touched with genuine love or affection? How long since someone had cared at all? She'd been locked away half a lifetime. Wasted years that could never be relived or re-captured. For the first time in her life, Jasmine wanted to lash out at fate for depriving her of the mother she'd always wanted.

The reminder of what they'd both lost made Jasmine angry enough to take another small risk. "I liked the song you were humming."

Lily ducked her head and rocked harder as if fearful and confused. "I don't know you."

Hoping she was doing the right thing, Jasmine crossed the room and opened the blinds a little. Then she turned to face the woman. "I'm Jasmine."

Her mother's face was pale, as if she hadn't been outside in years. There was a gentle innocence about her unwrinkled skin and a hint of perceptiveness in the green eyes that darted to Jasmine before fixing once again on the floor. That keen glance gave Jasmine hope.

Lily spoke softly in a singsong chant. "I like jasmine." At first Jasmine thought her mother was talking about her. But she was wrong. "The scent is so sweet, the bloom reminds me of…"

"Of what?"

Lily didn't respond to her question. She began to hum again.

As pleasant as the sound was, Jasmine preferred more conversation. "Do you like daisies?" She tried mentioning her deceased aunt's name in hopes of generating a memory.

"Flowers are precious."

"Would you like to walk outside? Maybe we might find some flowers," Jasmine suggested.

"Flowers are gone," Lily said sadly. "All gone."

As frustrated as she was by Lily's vague answers, Jasmine's hopes were high. They were communicating. Sort of. And maybe after Lily came to know her better, she'd speak more openly.

Jasmine had the distinct feeling Lily was being deliberately vague. Either that or Jasmine was hoping for the impossible. She couldn't expect too much, too soon. After two decades in this place, even a sane person would seem eccentric.

A woman in a nurse's uniform marched into the room, a frown on her face. Orange tufts of hair, reminiscent of Belle's, stuck out of her cap. Jasmine figured that distinctive color had to come from the same manufacturer.

"I'm Lily's nurse, Anne. Lily is not allowed visitors."

"Why not?" Jasmine asked.

The nurse shrugged her beefy shoulders. "Doctor's orders. You'll have to leave now."

Jasmine intended to search out Lily's doctor and find out why her mother wasn't allowed visitors. She also needed to find her medical records and ascertain Lily's diagnosis. Ignoring the nurse, Jasmine turned back to her mother. "Could we be friends? I'd like to come back and visit you."

"Why? There are no flowers here."

At the illogical response, Jasmine's neck prickled with worry. Now that she had found Lily, suppose they could never have a real conversation? She might have to accept that Lily would never be well enough to share her life.

And, oh, how she ached to share with her mother her good fortune of falling in love with Rand. But sensing that right now her mother wouldn't understand even a simple explanation about their relationship, Jasmine blinked away the tears in her eyes. "I'll come back tomorrow." With fresh flowers, a new dressing gown and a few magazines, she vowed.

Deep in contemplation, she hurried to the front entrance, barely noticing the patient in the baseball cap pacing the lobby. Tomorrow she would bring Rand back with her. They'd talk to the doctor in charge of her mother's care, find out exactly what was wrong with her—including why she'd been committed and was here under another name.

Rand would help. She knew he would. She'd be willing to bet her unsettled insurance claim that the receptionist would be much more helpful with Rand asking the questions.

As she shoved through the double doors of the lobby, the man with the baseball cap slipped outside, startling her. She'd assumed he was a patient, not a visitor. There was something furtive in the way he averted his eyes whenever she looked at him.

Could he be following her? Or was her paranoia working overtime? She was too emotionally drained to think and too tired to feel anything besides numbing regret and sorrow. Although she'd steeled herself against her pain that her mother hadn't recognized her, the years they'd lost of each other's company almost overwhelmed her.

But her mother had called her Sweet Flower. Enough self-pity. She'd never really expected to find

Lily alive. Her mother was still a young woman, and they would have many years together. Determined to get a grip on herself, looking forward to telling Rand about finding Lily, she hurried through the parking lot and halted on the sidewalk to cross the street.

The man in the baseball cap stopped beside her.

Chapter Ten

After finding her mother in such an awful state, Jasmine needed a breather. Yet since leaving the nursing home, she'd been almost positive that man in the baseball cap had been following her. She'd been so happy to see Art drive up to the curb, she could have kissed him.

The stranger had made no move to stop her from getting into Art's car. He had hurried on past at Art's arrival, and they'd driven away without incident. Her paranoid fear of the man in the baseball cap had been an overreaction.

Art had dropped her off at the hospital, and Rand took her back to Moore House. From the heated looks in Rand's eyes, she knew this time he intended to follow through on his kisses. And she couldn't wait.

LIKE NAUGHTY CHILDREN who'd missed an afternoon snack, Jasmine and Rand snuck into Belle's kitchen in search of an early dinner. Belle was nowhere in sight, Irene was off at one of her charity functions, Art, T.J. and Charles were still at work, while Blain was probably working on his tan.

Jasmine opened the refrigerator, and the glow lighting her blond hair reminded Rand of the silky strands brushing his shoulder and cheek, enticing him with the scent of clean soap and an essence that was pure Jasmine.

He'd never responded to a woman the way he had to her kisses, and he had ceased lying to himself, no longer denying the attraction between them was more than physical. Yes, she was a pretty woman, but he'd dated other women much more beautiful. None of them could turn him on the way Jasmine did with just an innocent look or passionate kiss. He couldn't wait to see if her responses were even more fervent in bed. And afterward, she'd fascinate him with the musical quality in her voice. He could talk to her for hours and never be bored or disappointed. She was everything he wanted in a woman.

But she knew so little about him. If only he could tell her the truth. God forgive him, he hated the lies. If she learned how he'd misled her, he could lose her so easily.

Once his secret was revealed, would she find a way to forgive him? Fear reared its ugly head. If she couldn't overlook his loyalty to the Moore family, he might find himself in the same situation as Dylan when Heather left him. Alone. Sad. Withdrawn.

Although Rand had tried to fight his feelings for Jasmine, he'd failed. Now he'd have to accept the consequences.

After he made love to her, if she left him, he'd yearn for her all the more. Although the thought of longing for her for the rest of his life was unthinkable, he planned to make love with her, anyway.

Jasmine pulled a foil-covered platter out of the

fridge. "There's cold turkey. How about a sandwich?"

"I'll bet it won't taste as good as you do."

He enjoyed the blush that crept up her neck to her face. She had never discussed past lovers, and he suspected there hadn't been many. He didn't need to know, didn't want to know. As far as he was concerned, tonight they were starting fresh.

She opened the bread drawer and took out a loaf of Belle's homemade sourdough. "There's something I have to tell you. Promise you won't be mad?" She opened another drawer and pulled out a serrated knife and sliced the bread.

He placed a hand over hers and gently laid the knife aside, determined to warn her before they made love. "I want to say something first."

She wound her arms around his waist and leaned back to look into his eyes. "What?"

"I've lied to you."

She remained silent, waiting for him to continue, waiting for him to explain. Only, explaining was impossible.

The silence grew taut.

He stared deep into her eyes. "I'm sorry. I still can't tell you. The truth will soon come out, but it's not my decision as to when that will happen. But I want you to remember this conversation. Remember that I had no choice."

Her beautiful face clouded with confusion. "I don't understand."

"I know." He bent and pressed his lips to her forehead. "When you're hurt by the lies, trust me enough to think that I did what I thought best. I put a prior obligation to...the Moore family first.'' His arms tightened around her, crushing her to him.

''You're scaring me.''

''I'm sorry. I'm apologizing too often.'' He released her and stepped away to collect his thoughts. When she'd trembled in his arms, he'd almost told her what lay in store for her. Just another few days, and she would know. He could put the lies behind him then.

Jasmine returned to making sandwiches, but the easy camaraderie they'd shared had vanished. He brought pickles, mustard, mayo and a pitcher of lemonade to the table. ''What were you going to tell me that I shouldn't be angry about?''

She must have sensed he wouldn't explain his cryptic remarks, because she shrugged and followed his change of topic. ''This afternoon, I went to Bayside Hospital.''

''Alone?''

''Art took me. And nothing dangerous happened except a man that I thought was a patient followed me out of the building. But he was harmless.''

''Whoa. Slow down. Why don't you start at the beginning and tell me everything.''

As they ate their sandwiches, she told him about finding her mother. He had difficulty believing her story. But as she piled fact upon fact, she convinced him she really had found Lily Ross. His heart swelled with happiness that she had overcome so many obstacles and gotten what she wanted.

Jasmine's incredible story brought the glow back to her face that had disappeared when he'd admitted he'd lied to her. Her bright eyes sparkled as she explained that Lily Ross was listed as Lily Smith, but she'd identified her mother from the music box tune, her profile, her calling Jasmine by a childhood nickname and her tears after Jasmine mentioned Talbot's name.

"Can you come with me tomorrow when I visit?"

"I'll be glad to. I would have been with you today, but I had to check on Joe."

"How is he?"

"His doctor thinks he'll retain full use of his arm." He poured them both some lemonade. "Tomorrow, I'll be free to go with you to visit your mother. I'd like to know who's been paying Lily's bills all these years. Bayside is private and expensive."

"I want to take her flowers. And the music box."

"Good idea. I'm sure she'll like that. But I don't want you to be disappointed. You must realize Lily may never..."

"Be normal?"

"Recover."

"I know." Jasmine sighed, the last of her sandwich evidently forgotten. "She seemed so sad. Surely her life will be better knowing that someone cares about her, that someone loves her?"

"I'm sure it will. Just remember, she's probably been institutionalized for a long time."

He rinsed his dish in the sink while Jasmine stared at her plate. When he scraped her sandwich into the trash and placed her dish in the sink, she didn't appear to notice. The meeting with her mother had left her thoughtful. He wished she'd waited for him to have gone with her.

He gave her a few minutes to think while he rewrapped the platter of turkey and put it in the fridge. She sent him an unreadable glance while he wiped up the crumbs. "Belle will have my head if she learns we ate tomorrow's lunch."

He expected Jasmine to smile, but her face remained serious. "Why don't you go on up and start your shower while I take out the trash?"

She suddenly flashed him a devastating smile, and he realized her thoughts hadn't been on her mother at all. "You've got five minutes, mister."

JASMINE REMOVED HER clothes and laid them neatly on the towel rack before turning on the shower. Despite her teasing words to Rand, her thoughts were troubled. Hoping warm water would soothe her frayed nerves, she waited for the temperature to heat. She had so much on her mind. She didn't like Rand lying to her. Judging from the anguish in his eyes, he didn't like it, either. The only reason she hadn't pressed him was because she trusted him. And she had more than enough to worry about. Between finding her mother, unexplained puzzles at Moore House and someone who wanted her dead, she was a wreck, but recalling the look in Rand's eyes when she left the kitchen, she cast all worries from mind.

No sooner did she step into the private shower off her bedroom than she heard footsteps in her room. Glancing over her shoulder through the partially open shower door, she spied Rand making a beeline for her. At the anticipation in his eyes, her heart thudded.

Instinctively, she knew their lovemaking would be wonderful. How could it not be when Rand was so wonderful? She envisioned big fluffy towels, crisp linen sheets, privacy under the canopy of the four-poster bed.

He opened the shower door, and she pretended he wasn't there. Instead, she tilted her face up to the spray and arched her back, hoping to entice him.

"Wow!"

"See anything you like?" she asked, with a boldness that still surprised her. But just being with him gave her a confidence she'd never had before. At Rand's appreciative whistle, she cast any embarrassment aside.

He grinned. "I feel like a kid in a candy store that wants to sample two of everything."

"Come on in. The temperature's just right."

Rand reached into his back pocket and slapped his wallet on the counter. He stepped out of his shoes, stripped and stepped into the shower. In a moment, he was drenched, water droplets skimming his broad shoulders and chest.

He stepped behind her and reached for the strawberry soap, letting her hog the spray. "I couldn't wait another moment."

Aroused by the huskiness in his voice, she quelled her cautious side. "Have a sweet tooth, do you?"

He nipped the sensitive spot between her shoulder and neck, his voice low and husky. "I think I've died and gone to candy heaven. There's only one problem."

She glanced over her shoulder at him and caught a mischievous sparkle in his eyes. "What?"

"With the luscious delicacy before me, I can't decide where to start."

A tingle shimmied straight to her heart. Ah, how she loved this man. He believed in her with a faith that made her heart swell. She couldn't wait for him to touch her. But despite his hurry to jump into the shower, he seemed in no great rush.

Instead, he devoured her with his eyes, taking in every swell and hollow of her back and buttocks, while he worked up a lather of soap in his hands and strawberry scents mixed with steam.

"Rand?"

"Umm?"

"Come here. I want to kiss you."

"Not yet. All afternoon, I've been looking forward to washing you." His hand rested on the sensitive spot of her shoulder where he had nipped her, his thumb circling in a delicate caress. He lifted her hair off her neck and planted a row of kisses along her nape that sent shivers down her spine. "What an adorable heart-shaped birthmark."

"Aunt Daisy told me the birthmark runs in our family and skips generations. My grandmother had one, too."

"Mmm. All afternoon, I imagined running soap over skin slick with water droplets." He cupped her bare bottom and her breath left her on a delicious whoosh. She needed to kiss him, needed to touch him.

But when she started to turn, he swatted her bottom. "Stand still. How will I get you clean if you keep squirming?"

"Clean isn't want I want."

"Really?"

When his fingers trailed upward instead of downward, she bit back a groan of frustration. "Rand—"

"You don't know what you want."

Oh, yes she did. She wanted him. Now. And he was prolonging their separation. From his cocky tone, he knew exactly what he was doing. Setting her on fire. She ached to push away his seductively slow hands, spin and demand a kiss.

Her back arched, her breasts peaked, begging for his touch. With lathered fingertips he reached around her and caressed her breasts. Her flesh prickled, mirroring the excitement bubbling inside and threatening to explode. Biting her lower lip to restrain a whimper, she leaned against his muscular chest and let his hands roam as he pleased.

"You're going to pay for this."

"I look forward to it."

"I need more," she half whispered, half pleaded, crazy with desire.

"Yes," he promised. Driving her crazy, he continued to run his hands over her until she bucked upright.

"Enough. You have to stop teasing me."

"I know."

As if she hadn't said a word, he found her breasts again, touching, taunting until she ached to cry out at the tension stringing her taut as a quivering string.

Wrenching away, she twisted to face him until her breasts pressed to his chest and her face was just inches below his. She had to touch him, feel his bare flesh against her own.

Still he wasn't close enough. "Kiss me," she pleaded, wanting to taste him, trying to draw him to her.

He stepped back, bent and took a nipple into his mouth with tantalizing possessiveness. She'd expected him to kiss her on the mouth. But she couldn't deny the pleasure of his tiny nips, followed by erotic licks that made her senses reel as if short-circuited.

Legs weakened by his heated onslaught, she leaned against the cool tile.

This was madness. And she was loving every minute of it. But she couldn't take much more.

"Please. You have to stop…"

"Yes."

He parted her trembling thighs. An exhilarated growl rose from his throat as he slipped his fingers inside her. Her skin tingled where he touched her. Back braced against the tile, she thrashed, helpless to do more than bite back a scream.

When he shifted his mouth to the sensitive spot where his fingers had been, she cried out in pleasure.

He cupped her bottom, his mouth to her core, holding her captive, his hot breath against hotter skin.

She shook her head back and forth. Wild. Needy. "I can't…take…"

"You can."

She moved her hips, restless, eager. She buried her hands in his thick hair. His touch brought back a ripple of emotions that hammered her heart, singed the corners of control and urged her toward the brink of a need so fierce she barely recognized it as desire. Her breath shortened to choppy gasps, until the heady sensation of his lips against her sent her spinning out of control into a wondrous climax. She might have fallen if he hadn't carried her to the bed.

Jasmine opened her eyes, marvelously sated. She was lying on her crisp cotton sheets, feeling a dreamy lassitude running through muscles so relaxed it was an effort to keep her eyes open.

Rand gazed down at her, a worried and tender frown on his face. "You all right?"

"Never better." Jasmine let out a contented sigh

and lay back on the fluffy pillow. She smiled and stretched her arms over her head like a lazy cat, then patted the empty spot beside her on the bed in invitation.

Rand slipped into bed beside her. He drew her gently against his chest, cradled her head as he threaded his fingers through her hair. "You sure you're okay?"

She crushed him to her and bit her lip to restrain a happy moan. She might be light-headed, her heart might be beating too fast with her pulse twice its normal rate, but what she needed was Rand, holding her, cuddling her, letting her get drunk on the sweet power of love.

But love was a two-way street, and he had yet to reach satisfaction.

Rolling to her side, she bent her arm and rested her head in her palm. She could look at him for hours. She adored watching the light angle across his tanned skin. "Umm, Rand? You do remember what I said about getting even?"

He lifted her free hand and planted a kiss in her palm. "You should rest."

"Not a chance."

In the soft glow of the late afternoon sunlight streaming through her windows, his hair glistened like polished black glass. His dark eyes smoldered with a sensuality enhanced by tiny droplets on long, dark lashes. The inherent strength in his face, compelling gray eyes, slanted cheekbones and square jaw was tempered by a mouth touched by tenderness.

She trailed her fingers over the muscles of his chest, to his flat stomach, lower. His sex was very evident…and arousing.

She eyed him up and down covetously. "Now that I have you exactly where I want you—I intend to take advantage."

She grazed the tips of her fingers along his erection while staring directly into his eyes.

He reached for her and she gently took his hand and put it beside his head. "My turn."

He laced his fingers behind his head with a groan. "You don't play fair."

"Oh, I know the rules of this game," she teased.

His eyes narrowed in resigned suspicion. "And they are?"

"No mercy."

BELLE HAD DISAPPEARED.

Irene informed them Belle had taken her belongings and gone away without leaving so much as a note. Charles was furious that he'd had to go out for breakfast. Art and T.J. took the cook's vanishing act in stride, while Blain, probably oblivious, had yet to waken after a late night at the beach.

Rand had been oddly silent about Belle's absence. Jasmine well knew how the unexplained disappearance of a loved one could upset those left behind. Suspecting Belle and Rand had been closer than he'd admitted, she followed Rand's lead. When he didn't say much, she let the subject drop.

And in truth, the puzzle of Belle's disappearance couldn't compete in her thoughts with having finally found Lily. After all the years of wondering what had happened, she sensed herself on the verge of answers.

With Rand at her side to give her strength, she couldn't fail to solve the last pieces of how and why her mother had ended up at Bayside. Her stomach fluttered every time she looked at the handsome, self-assured man beside her and recalled the way he'd made love to her. She hugged the delicious memory to herself, had to restrain her feet from skipping into Bayside.

As they approached the front desk, the female receptionist from the day before was nowhere in sight. Instead, a pleasant-faced man greeted them. "May I help you?"

"I'd like to speak to the hospital administrator, please," Rand said.

"That would be Dr. Albright. May I say what this is concerning?"

Jasmine squeezed Rand's hand. "One of your patients, Lily Ross. But you have her listed as Lily Smith."

The man closed his ledger, then pressed his intercom. "Dr. Albright, two people would like to see you about a Lily Smith or Lily Ross."

"Show them in, please."

Dr. Albright's office took advantage of the morning light. The bright room, painted in a cheerful shade of pale yellow, had an optimistic atmosphere. Even the perky potted palm beneath numerous framed degrees that lined one wall seemed welcoming.

Dr. Albright stood behind a massive desk and greeted them in a gracious tone. "Good morning." After introductions, he offered them seats. "What can I do for you?"

"My mother disappeared when I was a child," Jasmine began. "I had no idea if she was even alive until yesterday when I visited here. Lily is one of your patients."

"Her full name?" Dr. Albright asked.

"Lily Ross, but the name on the door of her room said Lily Smith."

Dr. Albright checked his computer records, frowned, then leaned forward and regarded her intently. "I'm sorry. We have no patient here by either of those names."

Rand cleared his throat. "There must be a mistake."

"I don't think so. Our records are meticulous. If you want, you can check for yourself," Dr. Albright offered. "Perhaps you visited the county sanatorium?"

"This is ridiculous. I was here." Jasmine turned to Rand. "You can ask Art where he dropped me off."

"Take it easy," Rand said. "I believe you."

His soothing voice didn't calm her. They could solve the record-keeping problem later. In the meantime, she wanted to see Lily. "My mother was in room 105." Jasmine jumped to her feet. "Come on. I'll show you."

Dr. Albright walked with them down the corridor. "We've never lost a patient before."

Rand put his arm around Jasmine's shoulders. "Computer errors can happen. But aren't you familiar with all the patients in this facility?"

"I'm afraid not." Dr. Albright removed his glasses, then replaced them on the bridge of his nose. "I'm new here."

"How new?" Jasmine asked.

"I started at Bayside this week. The former director died rather unexpectedly."

"How did he die?" Rand's tone remained casual, but Jasmine sensed his tension by the tightening of a muscle in his jaw.

"Some kind of car accident, I believe. So you see, my appointment was rather sudden. And we have more than three hundred patients. While I've tried to see everyone, administrative duties keep me busy."

Jasmine made a mental note to find out exactly how the former administrator had died. Perhaps his death was simply a coincidence. Maybe her paranoia was flaring up. But Rand seemed almost as suspicious as she was.

If only Lily could tell them what she knew. They had to learn why her mother was here, the circumstances of her admittance and who was paying her bills. In her heart, Jasmine suspected Talbot Moore had something to do with her mother's disappearance all those years ago—but she had no proof. She could no more question her deceased father than she could have questioned her mother yesterday, in her fragile mental state.

Jasmine especially wanted to talk to the doctor who treated her. As they neared the room, irrational hopes of eventually getting answers from her mother increased.

Would her mother remember her from yesterday's visit? Would she appreciate the bouquet of fresh flowers Jasmine had brought her?

As they turned a corner, Jasmine glimpsed the patient who had led her to her mother's room yesterday. She was wearing the same robe and slippers and sat on one of the numerous benches lining the hallway.

As they neared, Jasmine waved. "Hello."

"Is that your mother?" Rand asked.

"That's Ava Baumgartner," Dr. Albright said.

Jasmine slowed as they neared the woman. "She

brought me to Lily's room after the receptionist couldn't find the name in her computer.''

The patient refused to look at Jasmine. She stared at her sleeve, picking at a loose thread, obviously oblivious to their presence.

''I never got a chance to thank you yesterday.'' On impulse, Jasmine plucked a blue carnation from the bouquet and offered the flower to the woman.

When the patient refused to look at her, Dr. Albright took the flower and placed it across her lap. ''She had a flare-up this morning and she's been medicated.''

Jasmine frowned. ''Yesterday she seemed fine.''

Dr. Albright shrugged philosophically. ''We all have good days and bad days.''

Jasmine's anxiety to see her mother increased. She hoped Lily could speak to them at least as coherently as yesterday. If her mother had regressed as much as Ava, Jasmine would be devastated.

Today, the door to room 105 was shut. The name tag had been removed, but she was so eager to see her mother again, Jasmine didn't let a missing name tag deter her. After so many years spent apart, leaving her yesterday had been difficult. But she hadn't wanted to overwhelm her mother, either.

''Knock, knock,'' Jasmine said, her voice light. ''Can we come in? It's Jasmine, and I've brought Dr. Albright and a good friend of mine.'' Feeling silly talking to the closed door, she felt even more foolish saying Rand was a mere friend. But she was trying to keep things simple.

She looked over her shoulder at the two men. ''She didn't answer after I knocked yesterday, either.''

With a turn of the knob, Jasmine opened the door. The room was dark. Rand flicked on a light.

Oh, god! No.

Jasmine's knees buckled. Only Rand's steady support kept her on her feet. This couldn't be happening. Not again. Not here.

The patient's room of yesterday was today's storage room, stacked from floor to ceiling with furniture. Her mother was gone.

Chapter Eleven

Rand only glanced at the crowded storage room before he focused on Jasmine. The color drained from her face, leaving her eyes looking overlarge and haunted with agony. Hoping to ease her through her disappointment, he took one of her icy hands into his and remained alert and ready to catch her in case she collapsed.

"My mother *was* here yesterday." Jasmine's voice trembled with heartbreaking uncertainty. "You believe me, don't you?"

Rand nodded. "Perhaps you have the room number wrong. Are you sure you weren't in 205 or 305, or you reversed the numbers in 501?"

"There is no fifth floor," Dr. Albright said.

"I didn't climb stairs or take an elevator," Jasmine confirmed.

"Well, then perhaps you mixed up this corridor with another. These hallways look alike." Rand couldn't begin to imagine her pain. He yearned to embrace her, smooth her hair and tell her everything would be all right, that they'd find her mother. But he wasn't so sure. Someone was one step ahead of them.

This was the first time one of these odd, puzzling incidents had occurred outside Moore House.

From the look of her, swaying like a palm tree during a hurricane, Jasmine might be on the verge of a breakdown.

But she straightened her back, squared her shoulders and spoke forthrightly. "Yesterday, I came straight to this room from the reception desk, and Dr. Albright's office is next door. There's not much chance I've become turned around."

"Everyone occasionally gets lost." Rand tugged her closer to his side. "Let's check the rest of the facility."

"This is highly irregular," Dr. Albright protested. "Our patients are entitled to their privacy."

"But under the circumstances," Rand argued, "I hope you'll give us a little slack."

They searched the busy game area where the patients played cards and bingo, the cafeteria and the media room. Jasmine knocked on doors of each room and spoke to every patient on all four floors. Their search proved futile. The woman Jasmine thought was her mother wasn't here.

On the way home, Rand tried to stir her out of her misery by engaging her in conversation. "Yesterday, before you visited, did you tell anyone where you were going?"

Jasmine shook her head, which rested against the seat, her eyes closed as he drove. "I didn't decide to go to Bayside until after I realized you'd be at the hospital with your injured employee. Art was the only person who knew my destination. And he didn't even come inside with me."

"What about after you saw your mother? Did you tell anyone you'd found her?"

"I wanted to tell you first. No one was home when we returned—not even Belle," she reminded him.

Rand had forgotten. When he'd spared thoughts about yesterday, he'd dwelled on their lovemaking rather than the preceding events. Rather than allow the pleasant subject to dominate his thoughts, he forced himself to stay on topic. "Does Belle's disappearance on the eve of your mother's vanishing act seem odd to you?"

Jasmine's eyes flew open. "What are you implying?"

"I'm not sure." Rand turned off the four-lane highway toward town. "After working a lifetime for the Moore family, why would Belle steal away in the middle of the night without explanation?"

Jasmine had no answer, and said nothing further until he parked in front of the Dolphin Bay Police Department. She frowned at him. "Do you think Dylan will help?"

Rand hoped she had the strength for police questions. God, how he longed to release her topknot, thread his fingers through her hair until it brushed her shoulders. But after last night, he wouldn't be satisfied with just a touch or a kiss. If only he could confide in her. Keeping secrets could be more of a curse than a blessing. With a mountain of regret, he grappled with his last bit of restraint and opened the car door. "I thought you'd want to fill out a missing person report on your mother."

"Don't I have to wait twenty-four hours?"

"There are extenuating circumstances here. Your mother was a patient in a mental hospital."

He made the ordeal as easy as possible for her. After the police took their information, they drove back to Moore House. They entered her bedroom together. The drapes were drawn shut, and Rand switched on the lamp beside the bed, swiftly checking to ensure her room was safe, as had become his habit. Behind him, Jasmine gasped.

Tensing, expecting danger, Rand spun.

One tear trickling down her delicate cheek, she pointed to the nightstand. Anguish reflected in eyes huge with horror. "Who would do such a thing?"

The music box, her only link with her mother during all those lonely years, was now no more than splintered and smashed slats of hammered wood.

Rand gathered her into his arms and gently tugged her head until their gazes locked. "I'm sorry. I know how much the music box meant to you. But we're in this together. I love you."

At his declaration, her eyes brimmed with tears.

He kissed her brow, her nose, her mouth. "Everything's going to be all right."

"JOE'S TAKEN A TURN for the worse," Charles told Rand through the door of Jasmine's bedroom.

Sleepily, she opened her eyes against the bright morning sunlight. Rand, beside her on the bed, slipped from beneath the quilt and yanked on slacks. "I told the surgeon to fly in a specialist."

"They already have," Charles said. "But you need to go to the hospital and sign some papers since the insurance won't cover—"

"Give me a minute and I'll be downstairs."

Charles's footsteps receded, and Jasmine sat up, her head pounding. Nightmares about losing her mother had interfered with her sleep. Despite the security of Rand's arms and his wonderful statement that he loved her, she'd wakened with a start at least twice during the night. She suspected he hadn't slept well, either, but if he could rouse himself to go to the hospital, so could she. "I'll come with you."

He glanced her way and shook his head. "You look exhausted. Charles can stay at the house and watch over you until I get back."

Not only was Rand generously paying medical expenses the insurance company wouldn't cover for his employee, he remained unfailingly kind to her. He'd disposed of the ruined music box so she wouldn't have a constant visual reminder of her loss. Rand had even called Dr. Mason and questioned the psychiatrist about Bayside Hospital and Dr. Albright's reputation. And he'd encouraged her to fill out a missing person report on her mother with the police.

Despite all evidence to the contrary, not once had he doubted her story. Rand Sinclair's love was the one thing she could count on in this uncertain world. Without his strength, she'd be lost.

He kissed her on the mouth before leaving. "I'll miss you."

"Miss you, too."

Jasmine had just drifted off to sleep when a loud knock on the door startled her wide awake.

"Who is it?"

"There's an officer downstairs in the study who wants to speak with you," Charles said.

Hoping Dylan Wade had learned more about the fire and the arsonist, Jasmine leapt out of bed, her thoughts on the insurance company's settlement.

She'd never intended to live off the Moore family's charity. "I'll be right down."

Five minutes later, she'd pulled on a pair of jeans and a clean blouse, brushed her teeth and hair and splashed cold water on her face to finish waking. Pushing open the study door, she entered the stuffy room, disappointed to find Dylan wasn't waiting for her. Instead, a brown-haired, blue-eyed officer whom she didn't recognize hesitantly stepped past Irene and Charles.

"Is Rand all right?" she asked, fearing a car accident.

"He's fine," Irene assured her.

Jasmine let out the breath she'd been holding and forced air into her lungs. "Have you found my mother?" Jasmine asked the officer.

"No, ma'am. I'm—"

"You've found the arsonist?" Jasmine wondered why he appeared so reluctant to come to the point.

The officer smoothed his shirt cuffs and refused to meet her eyes. "No, ma'am, I'm here on another matter entirely. Are you Jasmine Ross?"

"Yes." She glanced at Charles, but his kindly face was scrunched in a frown. While he looked as puzzled as Jasmine felt, Irene's face was pale. Her hands shook.

The officer spoke to Jasmine. "You'll have to come with me, ma'am."

"Why?"

Oh, God. Were they arresting her for the fire that had burned down her house? Her thoughts raced, but outwardly she forced calm.

"I have orders to take you down to the County Crisis Center."

Her mouth was dry and dusty like old paper. "I don't understand."

Irene patted her shoulder awkwardly. "Neither do I."

Fidgeting with the collar of his uniform with one hand, the officer offered her an official-looking document. "You've been Baker Acted."

Irene let out a screech. "Charles, do something."

Jasmine had never heard the term *Baker Act* and turned to Charles for an explanation. "Baker Acted?"

"Under whose authority is the order signed?" Charles asked, stepping protectively in front of her. "When was the document enacted? Who instituted these proceedings? Are the signatures legal?"

The officer shrugged. "That paper should explain."

Charles took the paper from the officer. "Dr. Mason has committed Jasmine to a psychiatric center."

Jasmine sputtered, too stunned and confused to speak. Her breath burned in her throat. She fought off a sickening wave of dizziness.

"This is for your own good," the officer told her. "I don't want any trouble."

Jasmine leaned around Charles, but with tears brimming in her eyes she couldn't focus on the tiny print. Refusing to yield to the compulsive sobs that shook her, she rigidly held her tears in check. "What does it say?"

"Dr. Mason signed the order," Charles explained. "Danger to yourself, suicidal gesturing, delusional, psychotic behavior. The order mentions your calling the fire department unnecessarily and reporting a false missing person report with the police department."

She tried to hide her inner misery from Charles's

sympathetic stare. A sickening suspicion that Rand had set her up caused her to teeter on her feet. "But my room was full of smoke. Any reasonable person would have called 911. And Rand encouraged me to file the missing person report."

The doctor Rand had recommended was sending her to a mental hospital, the same doctor Rand had spoken to on the phone yesterday. She'd thought he'd been trying to avoid disturbing her rest by speaking in a voice so low she couldn't hear his words. Could he have been betraying her?

Charles gave her a quick hug. "I'm so sorry. There's nothing I can do. The document is legal."

"Did *you* have anything to do with this?" Jasmine asked Irene, who looked pale enough to faint. But Jasmine was in no mood to tiptoe around Irene's feelings. The woman looked guilty.

Irene's lower lip trembled. She burst into tears, let out a sob and shook her head.

Jasmine didn't know what to make of her. The woman always overreacted.

"I think…" Charles hesitated, then pressed his lips firmly together as if refusing to say more.

"What?" Jasmine asked.

"Tell her," Irene sobbed.

Charles sighed. "But I'm not certain. I refuse to make unfounded accusations without proof."

"It must have been Rand," Irene gasped out, then fled up the stairs.

Rand?

Jasmine had considered his behavior suspicious from the start of their relationship, but had thought he really loved her. She'd wanted to believe him so badly, she'd fooled herself. Even now, she had difficulty thinking disparagingly of him. He'd been so kind, understanding, loving. Had his behavior all been an act?

How could Rand have done this to her? Her head swirled with doubts. How could Rand have been so cruel to pretend to believe every word she'd said only to commit her to a mental hospital? She'd been a fool to trust him—but then, maybe he'd given her a warning.

Rand had told her in the kitchen that after she learned what he'd done she'd have to yield to his judgment. How his first obligation was to the Moore family. Like a ninny, she hadn't taken his warning seriously. She should have run far, far away and never come back. Instead, she'd made love to him with her heart open wide, unaware of her perilous circumstances.

Had Rand ever felt anything for her at all? Had his every word been a lie? Bitterness welled up in her throat, choking her.

Maybe she *was* crazy. She couldn't explain her mother's disappearance, couldn't prove she'd seen the warning note or Talbot's chest in the attic that had mysteriously shown up in Irene's room. She'd heard strange laughter in her bedroom that had never been explained. Unlocked doors had locked, the missing key turning up on the music box. No one else could confirm her experiences. Maybe she belonged in a nut house.

Panic welled up inside her.

Rand's betrayal tore at her battered soul. Floundering in despair and doubt, she fought to remain composed, but inside a wretchedness consumed her. Rand thought she was crazy. The knowledge twisted inside her. Crazy like her mother. They would lock her away.

The officer gently took her forearm. "Are you on any medication, ma'am?"

"No."

"Please come quietly."

Anguish caused her to stumble. Her knees buckled. Only the officer's firm grip on her arm kept her from falling. The world went black. The next thing she knew, she was in the back seat of the police car, slumped against a seat belt.

She would end up like her mother, drugged, confused, hopeless. Her friends would think she'd forgotten them. No one would look for her, certainly not her new family. T.J. hated her. Art wouldn't cause trouble, and Blain wouldn't notice. Irene would probably be pleased the scandal had been swept under the rug, and Charles would defer to Irene's wishes.

Rand probably wouldn't give her another thought. He'd run the family business, with full majority control as he wanted. With a moan of distress, she recalled how he'd lied to her from the start. She'd heard men's voices on her first visit to Moore House and later in Rand's room. She recalled Rand locking her into her room before Blain set the fire. He could have deliberately switched the key. And Rand was the only person she'd told about finding her mother. She'd never forgive him for pretending to search the entire facility when he'd obviously sent her mother elsewhere.

Jasmine raised her hands to cover her face. She'd been a fool, taken in by an expert. For all she knew, the whole family might have been in on the plot together. And like a naive child, she'd fallen right into their trap. How could she have been so stupid?

Rand's betrayal left her feeling as if she'd been run over by a tank, every bone, hope and dream shattered. Damn him. She'd loved him. And he'd tossed her out like yesterday's garbage.

The car stopped in front of the County Crisis Center. Little by little, she became aware of her surroundings, the stench of stale sweat in the rear of the squad car, the rush of downtown traffic, the overwhelming realization that these next few hours might be critical to regaining her freedom and her life. She saw a familiar-looking man in a baseball cap in the Crisis Center parking lot. But she knew he wasn't the same man she'd seen at the hospital. She wasn't paranoid. She wasn't crazy. No matter how badly she was hurting, she had to concentrate, pull herself together to prove her sanity.

INSIDE THE COUNTY CRISIS Center, the police officer discharged Jasmine into the custody of Dr. Warren, an Asian-American woman with a no-nonsense attitude. She gestured for Jasmine to take a seat, then stepped around her desk in the cramped office.

Suppressing her spreading fears, shutting them in a dark corner of her mind, took almost more energy than Jasmine could exert. At the sound of doors locking behind her in the hallway, terror trailed her thoughts like a stalking shadow, doubts huddling at the edges, seeping into every crevice and cranny.

"Can you tell me your name?" Dr. Warren asked in a thick accent.

Feeling as if she were walking a tightrope over hell, Jasmine refused to give in to the panicky flutter of her heart, the pounding ache in her skull. "Jasmine Ross."

"Will you sign a paper to voluntarily commit yourself into our care?"

No way.

"How long can you keep me here if I refuse?" Jasmine trembled, vacillating between the need to cooperate and the need to wildly rant that she was sane. She had to hold herself together. She must. Or she could end up like her mother.

"Your stay depends upon how you do here."

"Good." Jasmine needed this doctor on her side. Right now, thankful for her own exceptionally organized mind that compartmentalized problems, she strove for logic. If she could overcome the horror of where she was, the antiseptic smell, the inhuman wails of other patients, the stinging loss of her freedom, she might yet talk her way out. Convincing Dr. Warren of her sanity with the evidence against her might be difficult, impossible, but she had to try.

The doctor asked Jasmine the date and who was president. After answering, Jasmine steeled herself, instinctively knowing the questions would become progressively more difficult.

Stay calm. Sound reasonable.

What should she say? Maintaining her composure was almost impossible with her freedom at stake. Not for one second could she forget the doctor could lock her in this facility and literally throw away the key.

Dr. Warren was bound to ask about her apparently delusional and paranoid behavior. Jasmine was tempted to lie, deny every incident. She wouldn't mention the man in the baseball cap whom she'd thought had followed her here today. But the doctor had other evidence before her that would refute her lies. Jasmine had called the fire department. Jasmine had filled out a missing person report with the police. Jasmine had trusted Rand, and he'd repaid her by sending her to the psychiatrist who'd had her committed.

Dr. Warren glanced down at a sheaf of papers. "Dr. Mason has prescribed medication for you."

"Drugs?"

"Yes."

"Can't I just say no?"

At Jasmine's joke, Dr. Mason smiled. "Do you think people are out to get you?"

Inwardly Jasmine flinched, outwardly she held still as stone. "Until someone burned down my house and business, I owned a computer school. Then I received a letter, which my mother had written to my father, that had been lost in the mail for twenty-five years." Sticking to the truth, Jasmine told Dr. Warren about her father's death in a fire, the odd incidents at Moore House and finding her mother, then her inexplicable disappearance. "So to answer your question, I don't believe *people* are out to get me. But I believe *someone* wants me out of the way. And they may have succeeded."

"Dr. Mason is very concerned about you. He's worried about the extent of your depression and that you've been thinking about hurting yourself."

"I have no idea how he could have formed that impression. I'm not depressed. I want to find my mother. Every moment I'm here…" Jasmine flushed as her voice rose an octave. For a moment, she'd lost control of the anger and hurt raging through her with the force of a summer storm. Collecting herself, she managed a bitter smile. ''I don't want to be here. When can I leave?''

''You've been Baker Acted. You'll be assigned a counselor. Dr. Mason will be in to see you. And you'll be given medication.''

An hour later, Jasmine had been forced to give up her clothes, her jewelry and her purse for a hospital gown. After locking her in a ward, an aide had shown her to a windowless cubicle with a hospital cot and a small bureau.

Jasmine collapsed on the cot, trembling, her stomach heaving. She'd been so hopeful she could talk Dr. Warren into believing her story. She'd been wrong. Just like she'd been wrong about Rand's love.

His betrayal had left her terrifyingly alone and vulnerable; her heart cracked as if she'd ripped open an artery and let the blood gush out. How could she have been so wrong about him?

Years of experience with computers had left her unprepared to read his gaze and touch. She'd staked her life that he'd believed her, that he'd been on her side. She couldn't have been more wrong.

A nurse entered the room with a paper cup full of water and two pills. ''Here's your medication, dear.''

For a moment, she actually considered giving up, letting the pills put her out of her misery.

Jasmine obediently took the medication. With her tongue, she shoved the pills between her upper molar and her gums, praying the woman wouldn't check her mouth.

''Open up.''

Jasmine did as she was asked, humiliated by the woman treating her like a child. If she didn't get out soon, she might go mad living in this place.

"Lift your tongue. That's a good girl."

The woman turned to leave and Jasmine spit the pills into her hand. The nurse turned back, an odd look on her face. For a moment, Jasmine feared she'd been caught.

But the woman reached into her pocket and pulled out a business card. "Oh, I almost forgot to tell you. There's a hearing tomorrow concerning your release. Your attorney will be there."

Jasmine's hopes skyrocketed. Had Charles found a way to get her out? "My attorney?"

"Yes." The nurse glanced at the card in her hand. "Randolph Sinclair III."

Chapter Twelve

Incarcerated in the County Crisis Center, Jasmine had found thinking impossible with her mind battered by exhaustion and her thoughts muddled with shock. During the long night, the recollection of finding her mother had faded to no more than a dim memory or a vaguely disturbing dream. An acute sense of loneliness had numbed Jasmine with the realization that everyone and everything she had once known was lost to her. Alone, enveloped by hospital-white walls, she'd curled into a fetal position, shut her eyes and mourned for a freedom now lost.

But this morning, her musings were as crisp as the fluorescent hospital lights, her grief packaged and tied inside her like a ticking bomb, ready to explode. As she followed the aide to the hearing room, Jasmine tried to ignore how vulnerable she felt wearing a hospital gown and slippers.

One thought filled her mind. Rand Sinclair. How dare he represent her when he'd put her there in the first place? Damn him. She hadn't even known he was an attorney. But that was minor compared to his other lies. She should have paid more attention when he'd looked so guilty that evening in the Moore House kitchen, his smoky eyes staring deep into hers.

Ever since, she'd been haunted by his damning words. *I've lied to you…I'm sorry. I still can't tell you…. But I want you to remember this conversation. Remember that I had no choice.*

She should have told him everyone had a choice. She should have insisted on the truth. But she'd been too anxious to make love, she would have forgiven him anything.

Not anymore. The extent of his betrayal was beyond comprehension, the agony slicing so deep, she had yet to shed a tear of release. If only she could forget his words. *When you're hurt by the lies, trust me enough to think that I did what I thought best.*

As if locking her from the world could ever be best. Anger washed over the hurt. Determination fueled her footsteps as she carried his message branded in her brain. *I put a prior obligation to…the Moore family first.*

At the time, she'd thought him noble. Now she knew better.

Straightening her spine, squaring her shoulders, she strode into the hearing room with as much courage and pride as she could muster in a hospital gown.

She found Rand, exuding a masculine confidence, his demeanor bordering on arrogance, talking to Dylan. His pewter gray eyes found hers, emitting a compassion so deep, a longing so raw that it camouflaged an all-but-hidden flicker of despair. She stopped where she stood.

Her brain whispered, Don't let him sway you with his tricks.

Her heart shouted, He loves you still.

The contradiction tore at her soul, clawing at her like a wild beast inflicting a mortal wound.

Rand hurried over to her. "Are you all right? Dylan and I came to get you out of here."

Had she been wrong? Or was she so in love with this man that she'd believe anything he said? She must be demented.

Before she could reply, Dr. Warren entered the room with an assistant. "Have a seat, please. I want to call this meeting to order."

Sitting beside Rand, Jasmine attempted to compose her wildly racing pulse, ignore how good he looked in a tailored sport coat and Brooks Brothers tie. She couldn't allow him to represent her or she might be stuck here. For a lifetime.

Knowing how rash her accusations would sound, she warned herself to be careful, but even mental patients had rights and were entitled to an attorney of choice. "May I say something?"

"You'll have your turn," Dr. Warren informed her, then faced Rand. "Mr. Sinclair, you've obtained a special judge's order to rush this hearing. While I admire your devotion to your client, as the admitting psychiatrist, Dr. Mason should be included in these proceedings."

"I'd like to speak with him myself," Rand said smoothly, but attuned to him, Jasmine heard the wintry anger beneath his matter-of-fact words. "Dr. Mason is out of town for two days. My secretary is trying to track him down. In the meantime, I have evidence that I believe you should hear."

Evidence that would probably keep her locked away forever, she thought morosely, wondering if she should interrupt and accuse Rand of duplicity. Locking her lips together to prevent herself from sounding strident and unstable, she fought down a howl of protest. No way could she charge him with deception without appearing paranoid.

"Go on," Dr. Warren ordered him.

"Records suggest this client is delusional and capable of harming herself."

Dr. Warren challenged Rand over the rim of her reading glasses. "Jasmine Ross claims to have seen her mother who disappeared twenty-five years ago."

Jasmine hated the way they were speaking about her as if she wasn't there. She'd found her mother. She knew it. Her only mistake was not taking her mother with her out of Bayside Hospital when she'd left.

Rand cleared his throat. "I've found Lily Ross, ma'am."

"What?" Jasmine jumped to her feet, too astonished to maintain her self-control. Prepared for Rand's lies, she had never expected him to claim something so bizarre.

"Young lady, please be seated."

"Belle, the Moore family cook and housekeeper, phoned me yesterday. Apparently, Belle's sister, Anne, has cared for Lily Ross at Bayside Hospital for the last ten years. The old administrator had left orders that Ms. Ross's mother be moved and her room filled with furniture."

"I don't understand," Jasmine whispered, sinking back into her chair. Had she been wrong about Rand?

"I'll ask the questions," Dr. Warren said.

Rand had found her mother. The happy thought sank in slowly, and pure joy shot through her heart.

He hadn't betrayed her. He was fighting damned hard for her release.

A huge weight lifted from her shoulders. While she'd been blaming him for the worst treachery, he'd found Lily, brought Dylan to back his statements and obtained a special judge's order to obtain her release. Her heart swelled with love and mingled with a pang of guilt. She should have believed in him.

Dr. Warren leaned forward. "I don't understand, either. Explain, please."

Rand shrugged. "I don't have all the details. But we have a deposition from Anne that the woman Jasmine spoke to *is* Lily Ross. As the medication wears off, we hope her mother can tell us what happened so many years ago."

Dr. Warren winced. "Mental instability runs in the family?"

Jasmine held her breath, praying Rand had a good defense.

"No one's located Lily Ross's missing medical records. Several days ago, the former administrator of Bayside Hospital was killed."

Dylan, looking handsome in his police uniform, stood and placed a sheaf of papers on Dr. Warren's desk. "We've since learned the former hospital administrator was murdered in a fire that we first thought was an accident."

Dr. Warren frowned. "I'm sorry. You're losing me."

Dylan cleared his throat. "The significant fact is, the administrator died in a *fire*. Jasmine's father, Talbot Moore, was also murdered in a fire. And Jasmine's house was torched. I believe someone set out to make Jasmine appear mentally incompetent."

Dr. Warren was silent for a moment as she tapped her pencil on her desk. "Do you have proof?"

"Enough to know Jasmine Ross's life is in danger." Dylan planted his fists on the table and leaned forward. "Evidence from the fire marshall indicates the fire at her home was set by an arsonist—the same arsonist who killed Talbot Moore."

"Wouldn't she be safer in the hospital?" Dr. Warren asked.

Dylan shook his head. "With all due respect, security in this facility concentrates on keeping patients inside—not murderers out. Besides, if the arsonist is aware of Jasmine's whereabouts, her confinement could put the lives of other patients at risk."

Rand stood. "I'm asking you remand her into my custody so I can protect her."

"This is highly irregular. Dr. Mason—"

"I'll have him contact you. I want to know why he Baker Acted my client."

Dr. Warren glanced down. The room grew quiet. Finally she looked at Jasmine. "Your logical conduct during our interview combined with the new information brought here today has convinced me that while you may be in danger—it certainly won't be self-inflicted. I find you mentally competent. You are free to go."

JASMINE HAD NEVER appreciated her freedom enough. The sweet scent of sultry September air, the clean, bright sunlight filtering through scudding clouds and gently blowing palms, and the entrancing aroma of Rand's spicy aftershave helped her put the mental anguish behind.

After she'd thanked Dylan for his help and he'd

driven away, Rand stepped close and gathered her into his arms. "I'm sorry the doctor I recommended had you committed. I still don't understand what happened. Dr. Mason is at a conference in Tampa for the day. As soon as my secretary tracks him down, she'll phone."

Unable to deny herself the indulgence, she snuggled against Rand's powerful chest, buried her face against his neck, feeling blissfully elated he'd come to her rescue. She suddenly wanted him with an intensity that shook her. She wanted his arms to shield her from the horror of the Crisis Center, wanted his kiss to wash away the last remaining bitter taste in her mouth.

He bent his head, lips meeting hers. She gasped at the unexpected rightness of his hands cradling her back. She reveled in the warmth of his mouth, inhaled the enticing scent of his flesh, stroked one finger down the hard line of his cheek and neck.

Swallowing back a moan of bare pleasure, she sampled the heat of his mouth with hunger and undeniable need.

"You taste so good," he said thickly as he took her mouth again. "So damn good."

As Rand coaxed her tongue to mate with his, every nagging doubt she'd ever had about him boiled to vapor and floated away on the breeze.

Content in his arms, she pulled back just enough to see his face. "You don't think I'm crazy?"

"No, but *I* am—about you."

One look into his heated gaze and satisfaction that he spoke the truth flowed through her. "How did you find me?"

Slowly, reverently, he released her. "Another phone call."

She frowned at Rand's vague reply. But what did it matter whether Irene or Charles had called him? After Rand had just rescued her, she was not about to start doubting him again. Let him keep his secrets.

Rand took her hand, led her to his car and changed the subject. "I have a gift for you." His expression tender, he reached into the car, retrieved a cardboard box and handed it to her.

Tearing her gaze from the tender slant of his mouth, the heated glow in his eyes, she opened the container. And gasped. Inside was a music box, a replica of her mother's.

"Oh, Rand. How did you…?" She lifted the box's lid. At the familiar tune, her throat tightened.

"The mechanical insides were undamaged. The exterior wasn't salvageable, so I had a replica made."

Clutching the box in one hand, she wrapped an arm around him and pressed kisses to his lips and cheek. His thoughtfulness overwhelmed her. "Thank you."

He tangled his fingers in her hair, whispered softly in her ear. "I was afraid I'd never see you again." He tightened his grip, his voice husky. "I couldn't bear losing you."

After a long, satisfying kiss, he tenderly released her. "Would you like to visit Lily?"

Her heart buoyant with happiness, she nodded. "I'd like nothing better than to see my mother." She slipped into his car and waited for him to start the engine before he resumed the conversation.

"Belle and Anne are with Lily now. We'll be there in a few minutes."

Rand pulled into the shell drive of a one-story

frame house in an old but respectable neighborhood. "After Belle called, I moved Anne and Lily here."

"Where were they before?"

"A small apartment near the beach. Dylan is looking into who was paying rent on their former quarters. Apparently the landlord lives in Maine, and Dylan has been unable to reach him."

Music box in hand, Jasmine vacated the car, walked up the narrow sidewalk to the front stoop and knocked on the door. She half expected her mother to have disappeared again, but she said nothing to Rand about her fear.

Belle opened the door, her face sad. "Come in."

"My mother—"

"She's in the Florida room with Anne."

Thank goodness Jasmine's premonition had been wrong. For once, her mother was where she was supposed to be.

Rand followed Belle and her down the hall, giving Jasmine the opportunity to speak to the Moores' cook. "Thank you for calling Rand and telling him where to find my mother."

Belle grasped her hand and tugged her to halt, a curious look of fear on her face. "I also wrote the warning note."

Welling curiosity tinged Jasmine's tone. "Why the secrecy? Why didn't you just *tell* me my mother was alive?"

"First listen to my sister Anne's story, then I'll explain." Belle gave Jasmine a friendly shove down the hall. "You should know the new doctor Rand asked to examine your mother is weanin' her off the drugs. He says she's goin' to recover. She remembers her full name, but don't be expectin' much yet."

Jasmine and Rand walked into a sunny room with a picture window, an old lumpy couch and several unmatched pieces of furniture. Lily looked up from where she sat knitting on the sofa and waved. "Sweet Flower."

"Hello." Jasmine crossed the room and took a seat by her mother. "I told you I would return for a visit."

Lily stared at Jasmine, her eyes clouding with bafflement. "Anne said you are my daughter."

"Yes, Mama. I'm Jasmine."

Lily's lower lip trembled. "I don't remember."

Swallowing the lump in her throat, Jasmine set the music box on the coffee table, leaned over and embraced her mother. Frail and fragile in her arms, Lily shivered, and Jasmine ached for the lost years they could never regain. Resolutely she shoved the pain behind, refusing to dwell in the past. They had the future, and Jasmine wanted only happiness for her mother.

Gently, she patted Lily's hand and looked into her bewildered eyes. "I think maybe you do remember me. You keep calling me Sweet Flower. That was your pet name for me as a child."

"I always wanted a daughter," Lily said.

Jasmine had no way of knowing if her mother had understood her explanation. Over her mother's shoulder, Jasmine exchanged glances with Rand. He pointed to the music box and then to Lily.

She silently mouthed, *I love you.* Then she picked up the music box. "I have a present for you, Mama."

Lily opened the box with a show of excitement. As the familiar music started to play, her eyes sparkled. But she remained silent, staring at the wall and rocking.

Anne brought in a tray of iced tea and fresh-baked cinnamon rolls. Now that Jasmine had a chance to see Anne and Belle side by side, she realized their orange tufted hair was a dead giveaway they were sisters.

Anne placed the tray on the table. "Please, help yourselves. I imagine you have questions. Unfortunately I don't know too much."

Jasmine hoped Anne knew more than she thought. "How long did you work at Bayside?"

"For the last ten years. About the time you showed up at Moore House, I heard the former administrator talking to another man in his office behind closed doors. I'm not supposed to listen, but they were shouting about destroying Lily's records. After the administrator died so sudden-like, I got scared."

Jasmine sipped her tea to wet her parched throat. "And you told your sister?"

"Not exactly." She hesitated. "First Lily's records up and disappeared. Then I phoned Belle."

Belle shifted uneasily in a chair. "That's when I wrote the warning note."

"Why didn't you just tell me?" Jasmine asked, confused.

Belle shuddered. "I was terrified. Between Mr. Talbot's death, your house burnin' down and the hospital administrator's death in a fire, I knew that was too many accidents. I had to be careful. I sneaked back into your room and destroyed the note after I knew you'd read it."

Jasmine recalled how in the kitchen she'd questioned Belle about her mother and sensed the woman had been lying. No doubt Belle had been afraid. But she had tried to help her with the warning note.

Something wasn't quite right, and Jasmine didn't know what. Perhaps Belle's words sounded rehearsed.

Puzzled, Jasmine faced Anne. "Who was talking to the hospital administrator about my mother's records?"

Anne looked at Belle, then stared at the floor. "I don't know."

"Do you know who paid my mother's hospital bills?"

"No, ma'am."

Jasmine frowned. "Who arranged to move my mother from Bayside and have you accompany her?"

"The previous hospital administrator. The orders on his original paperwork were carried out."

Frustrated that every answer led to another dead end, Jasmine threw up her hands and almost gave up. "Did anyone ever visit my mother?"

"No visitors allowed," Lily said softly.

Jasmine wondered how much her mother knew and what she could tell them once she'd been weaned off the drugs. "Mama, I'll visit you every day. Would you like that?"

Lily didn't say another word. But she squeezed Jasmine's fingers so hard, her hand ached.

The two sisters hadn't given them much to go on. While Jasmine suspected they might know more, she couldn't force them to speak, and since they obviously wanted to help, she halted her questions before she started to sound like the Inquisition. Maybe tomorrow when she returned, they'd tell her more. Both would stay with Lily until Jasmine and Rand were assured of her mother's recovery.

After promising to return tomorrow, Rand escorted Jasmine back to his car. "Thank you for taking care of my mother.'' She gestured to the house. ''Someday, I'll repay you.''

''Don't think about that now.'' Rand opened her door. ''We need to figure out who has been taking care of Lily all these years.''

After Rand started the car, she turned to him. ''I thought Talbot might have been paying the bills. But unless he made provisions after his death…''

''That's possible. One of his sons or Charles may have carried through on Talbot's wishes. Or Irene could have continued to pay the bills and refused to tell us. Or she could have been paying them for years without Talbot's knowledge. With her, you never know.''

''What do you mean?'' Jasmine asked.

Rand threaded his fingers through his hair. ''Don't let Irene's hysterical behavior fool you. She's a very bright woman. She's also been treasurer of several large charity organizations and probably knows how to hide her financial tracks.''

Jasmine sighed. ''So now what?''

Rand gave her thigh an encouraging pat. ''Lily's stay in an expensive private hospital is suspicious, especially since she wasn't there under her own name. Someone was willing to pay her bills in the private facility rather than let her become a ward of the state. And now with her records lost and with the hospital administrator dead, someone has covered their tracks. But if we learn who has been paying your mother's bills, we may also learn who was behind committing you.''

''You don't believe that was simply bad judgment on Dr. Mason's part?''

''No way.'' Rand shook his head. ''But we need

proof. We'll go to Moore House and look through Irene's financial records. If we don't find payments to Bayside Hospital there, I'll check Charles's, Art's, T.J.'s and Blain's accounts, both business and personal.''

His determination and obvious belief in her lifted her spirits enough for her to mull over the problem. They might not know who they were looking for, but if they found canceled checks or receipts to Bayside Hospital, they would be on the way to solving a big piece of the puzzle.

It certainly seemed likely that whoever had torched her house was the same person who'd murdered her father. And it seemed even more likely that whoever had tried to commit her may also have had her mother put away twenty-five years ago. Only two people still living at Moore House were old enough to commit such crimes twenty-five years ago. Irene. And Charles.

Chapter Thirteen

"I need to go through your bank statements for the last year," Rand told Irene.

Irene paled and her eyes narrowed. "Have I overdrawn my account?"

Jasmine held her breath, sitting on the edge of her seat in the den at Moore House, waiting to see what Rand would do next. If she hadn't known him well, she might have mistaken his soft words for relaxed confidence. But his harnessed tension revealed itself in the clenching of a jaw muscle, the tightened cord of his neck, the soft, dangerous hum of his tone.

"I need to ensure your expenditures aren't exceeding the interest of Talbot's trust fund."

"Isn't that Art's job?" Irene twisted her hands. "After all, he is the accountant. Or are you taking that away, too?"

Looking as if he'd prefer to shake her, Rand folded his arms across his chest, displaying boundless patience. "What have I taken away?"

"Talbot spent his life building Sinclair and Moore. My sons are mere lackeys while you run the place."

Jasmine expected Rand to deny Irene's accusation.

She admired him when he spoke frankly, in a reasonable tone.

"I'd love for T.J., Art and Blain to take on more responsibility. They aren't ready," he explained gently to Irene. "Compared to the beach, the office has no appeal for Blain. Art prefers book work to getting his hands dirty in the field, and frankly, if T.J. spent less time worrying over you, he might concentrate more on business."

Irene slumped. "But Art is the accountant. I don't understand why you need to go through my personal account."

Jasmine had had enough of Rand's attempt to sweet-talk Irene. She stood and faced the woman who had objected to her staying at Moore House. "I found my mother living at Bayside Hospital. We want to examine your bank statements to see if either you or Charles has been paying her bills."

Irene bit her lower lip, her eyes darting wildly from Jasmine to Rand. "Lily is still alive? At Bayside?" Her chest heaved as she gulped in air. "Oh, my God. Did Talbot know?"

"Did you?" Jasmine asked.

"Of course I didn't know," Irene snapped, predictably bursting into tears. She reached into her purse and tossed her checkbook at Rand. "After all the years I spent being a mother to you, is this the thanks I get? How dare you accuse me—"

"Whoa. No one's accusing you of anything. But someone's been paying Lily's bills for years. We want to know who."

Irene backed toward the door, mascara mixing with her tears and running down her cheeks. "I don't want to know. I don't care. That woman wanted Talbot.

But he was mine. Now that he's dead, he'll always be mine.''

Irene slammed the door and pounded up the stairs. Rand stooped to retrieve the checkbook she'd thrown while Jasmine marveled at Irene's ability to throw a tantrum and upset everyone around her. While Irene had raised her voice, Jasmine's palms had broken into a sweat. Although Rand appeared to take her outburst in stride, Jasmine knew better.

"I'm sorry for telling her the truth and making your job more difficult." Jasmine went to Rand and put a hand on his shoulder. "By now I should have known she'd react to unpleasantness with hysterics. But with my mother's life and mine possibly at stake, we can't afford to tiptoe around her."

"I know." Rand shrugged, his eyes bleak. "Your apology isn't necessary. I suppose I let her get away with so much because I never felt close to her. If not for Talbot, I would have ended up in an orphanage or a foster home. I've tried to like her...."

"It's not your fault. Some people are too self-centered to be likable." Jasmine shuddered, thankful that she'd had Aunt Daisy, loving, kind Aunt Daisy, who had raised her with all the love Rand had never had. Her heart ached for him, and she vowed he'd never feel unloved again.

Rand flipped through Irene's check register, his face grim. "There's nothing here made out to Bayside."

Had they upset Irene for no reason? Guilt prickled at Jasmine. "Could she have another account, another checkbook?"

"It's possible." Putting the check register in his

shirt pocket, Rand took her hand. "Come on. Let's search Charles's office before he gets home."

"Without Belle to cook, surely he won't come back for lunch."

Rand shrugged. "For all we know, Irene is on the phone calling him right now. I don't trust her."

Rand's ominous tone sent a chill down Jasmine's neck and raised the gooseflesh on her scalp. While his arm wrapped over her shoulders, she sensed him pulling away from her emotionally and she didn't understand why.

She gazed at his closed expression. "What aren't you telling me?"

Stopping in the middle of the hallway, Rand tightened his arms around her with surprising intensity. Gently he lowered his head, kissed her forehead, cheeks and lips. Glancing into his troubled eyes, she caught a glimmer of uncertainty, and she recalled her vow to make him feel loved. Always.

She threw her arms around his neck, reveling in the honesty she saw fighting to come out. "I love you so much. I don't ever want to lose you. Please, Rand, whatever is wrong, tell me. We can face it together."

Stroking her back, Rand spoke softly. "Talbot was going to divorce Irene."

Shocked by his revelation, she leaned back and gazed into his smoky eyes. "How do you know?"

"Talbot and I were close. He told me he'd made a mistake marrying Irene. Now that his sons were grown, he wanted to end his marriage."

"Was Irene aware of his intentions?" In the short time Jasmine had known Irene, even she realized how devastated the woman would be at the loss of a husband. Now, instead of having to survive the aftermath of a messy divorce, Irene was the respectable grieving widow. An impending divorce cast a whole new perspective on Irene's possible involvement in Jasmine's troubles.

"Irene knew Talbot wanted a divorce," Rand said simply.

The ramification hit Jasmine like a slap in the face. "Then Irene had a motive for murder. She also had a motive to want my mother at Bayside—and me dead." She tried to keep the hurt from her tone. "Why didn't you tell me before?"

Rand caressed her chin. "For the same reason I probably shouldn't have told you now. I have no proof of Irene's motives. And considering my already cool feelings toward her, I tried to give her the benefit of the doubt. Besides, none of her sons are aware that Talbot intended divorce. Why shatter their illusions of their parents' happy marriage without good reason?"

RAND URGED JASMINE into Charles's office at Moore House and shut the door behind them. "While I go through Charles's desk, why don't you search his computer records."

Jasmine eased into the chair that dwarfed her. Rand wished he could solve the entire mystery for her while she stayed someplace safe. However, Dylan had insisted she'd be safest with Rand. Considering that she'd been locked in the Crisis Center last night, she'd held up surprisingly well. Wishing he could ease the frowns of worry at her brow and the tightly pursed lips, Rand turned to Charles's desk, knowing Jasmine's worries would end when they found out who was after her.

As he flipped through innumerable files, Rand considered what he would have done if he hadn't learned where Jasmine had been taken. He shuddered. Thank God he hadn't been forced to search for her in the hospital emergency room, or worse, the morgue.

Frantic with worry, he'd interrupted a judge during dinner to secure the paperwork for her morning hearing. Although satisfied she was now free, he didn't consider her safe. Until he found hard evidence to put whoever was after her behind bars, he wouldn't breathe easy again.

Jasmine sighed. "I'm no computer hacker. I can't get in without the password."

"It's 422CLK."

Jasmine typed. "I'm in. Thanks."

Rand found nothing suspicious in Charles's meticulously kept files. Grinding his teeth in frustration, he felt as if he was always one step behind Talbot's killer. As much as he wanted Jasmine to resume her normal life, a pang of dismay and regret seized him, leaving him with a terrible numbing fear. He could lose Jasmine after she learned of his lies. Would she hate him when she finally learned the truth?

Fighting to maintain his usual brisk efficiency, he shut the file drawer. Suddenly inspired to search more personal possessions, he strode to the closet, moved aside golf clubs and yanked down a carton from the top shelf.

"I'm scanning the files for a reference to Bayside." Jasmine stretched her arms over her head, rose to her feet and joined him. "Find anything?"

"Zip." Rand was digging through a box of sweaters when his cell phone rang. He punched a button and answered. "Hello?"

Rand leaned toward Jasmine and held the phone so she could hear. "Dr. Mason here. Your secretary said I needed to call you on an urgent matter."

"I want to know exactly why you committed Jasmine Ross." Rand made his tone hard, unpleasant.

"I'm not at liberty to divulge doctor-patient confidentiality."

Damn! Bluffing his way through the conversation, Rand tried intimidation. "I'm Jasmine Ross's attorney, and she's considering a malpractice suit. In case you haven't heard, my client was released from the County Crisis Center this morning after having been found mentally competent. In addition, the police are convinced her life may be in danger. Under the circumstances, I could have a judge issue a subpoena—"

"That won't be necessary." Dr. Mason caved in. "I ordered the Baker Act after Charles Wilcox called about her behavior. He was concerned that she could do damage to herself."

At his revelation, Jasmine stiffened beside him. The doctor spoke for a few more minutes about her separation from reality, but Rand barely listened, stunned that Charles had called Dr. Mason.

Had Charles really thought he was safeguarding Jasmine from suicide? He had always seemed so worried about her, overprotective. Rand had assumed Jasmine had raised Charles's paternal instincts, just as Irene had so long ago. Even as a child, Rand recalled incidents where Charles interfered in his sister's marriage, smoothing things over with Talbot. Perhaps Irene had leaned on Charles so much, she'd never grown up.

When Charles had appeared to treat Jasmine as he

did Irene, his interest had seemed natural and normal, in character. Could he really have believed she was better off in the Crisis Center? But if he'd had her committed out of concern, why hadn't he told her in advance? Why hadn't he discussed his concern with Rand?

Worse, if Charles's actions were malicious, why would he want Jasmine out of the way? Before Rand could mull over the implications of suspecting Charles, Jasmine's gaze sought his. "Charles could have had my mother hospitalized to get her out of the way so Irene could marry Talbot."

"It's possible."

Jasmine's eyes glowed with growing comprehension. "If Irene told Charles how upset she was about the pending divorce, he might have killed Talbot."

Charles? Not having known the man as long as he had gave Jasmine the advantage in seeing the facts unclouded by emotions. Unassuming, bland Charles? A killer? A psychopath?

"But why?"

Her fingers dug into his wrist in agitation. "Perhaps he was protecting his sister."

"Protecting her from what?"

"The embarrassment of divorce. Maybe she didn't want to split their assets. Perhaps she'd thought Talbot's will would leave her everything."

Slowly the facts coalesced as he put together what he knew. "Charles didn't know Talbot had made out that will. He *would* have expected Irene to get everything."

"Exactly. And if Irene got everything, Charles could control her and her fortune. Somehow Charles found out about my mother's lost letter and tracked me down. After I escaped the fire, he pretended to be my friend so he could make me appear crazy. Charles urged Dr. Mason to commit me. It all fits. It's even possible Irene and Charles planned the entire scheme together.''

Rand flexed his hands, raging at his own impotence. Without proof, all these logical deductions wouldn't get them anywhere. ''Too bad we don't have one shred of hard evidence.''

THE OFFICES OF Sinclair and Moore Construction hummed with activity. From the immaculate glass panels that overlooked a paved parking lot filled with employees' pickup trucks to the busy reception area, the business looked prosperous.

On the way to the office, Rand had called Dylan and asked him to meet them there. As he punched in another number, Jasmine's thoughts wandered. Had Charles sneaked into her room and opened the window, knowing the smoke from Blain's fire would fill her room? Had Irene arranged for Lily's former hospital room to be filled with old furniture? And who had returned Lily's lost letter to the mailbox?

A shudder rippled down her spine. If Charles and Irene had been lying to her from the start, it was no wonder she hadn't found answers. And the secret Rand had been keeping—that he knew Talbot had planned to divorce Irene, giving her a motive for murder—had thrown Jasmine off. Without vital clues, she hadn't known where to look. Through sheer determination and pure luck, she and Rand had found the partial letterhead with Lily's name in the attic that had led to finding her mother. One tiny scrap of paper overlooked after two and a half decades of lies. Whoever had paid her mother's bills had hid the tracks well. So far, neither she nor Rand had found any receipts, canceled checks or witnesses. The trail ended with a dead hospital administrator and a passel of unprovable conjectures.

As Rand led Jasmine down a tiled corridor past doors marked Bookkeeping, Estimating and Engineering, she faced the fact she and Rand might never be sure who was behind her mother's imprisonment and the fires. She might have to live with the distressing knowledge an arsonist would almost certainly make another attempt on her life, live with the frightening knowledge that someone in her family wanted her dead.

Rand barged into Charles's office without knocking. "We need to talk."

At the interruption, Charles dropped a leather briefcase onto his desk. A sheet of paper floated to the floor. "I was just leaving."

"This won't take long," Rand said.

Jasmine casually bent down and picked up the paper. She glanced down at it.

Face flushing to the tips of his ears, Charles held out his hand, palm up. "Let me have that."

Clearly the man was rattled. Jasmine shoved the useless handwritten travel itinerary into the back pocket of her jeans. "First tell me why you asked Dr. Mason to have me put away."

Charles made a visible effort to collect himself, but sweat beaded along his upper lip. "I don't have time for this discussion. Clearly, you are a danger to yourself."

"I'm a danger to you."

Charles rolled his eyes at the ceiling and turned to

Rand. "I don't know what she's talking about." He glanced at his watch. "I have a plane to catch. And I need the travel itinerary she—"

"You aren't going anywhere." Rand would have none of Charles's excuses. "If you were worried, why didn't you discuss Jasmine's mental state with me?"

Charles fidgeted with impatience. "You were too in love to see—"

Like a shark circling for the kill, Rand pressed Charles with a relentless tenacity. "Why didn't you call me after you'd had her taken away?"

She attempted to keep surprise from showing. She'd assumed Charles or Irene had told Rand where she was. But they'd remained silent? More and more circumstantial evidence pointed at either Charles or Irene. Still, she couldn't help wondering who *had* called Rand and notified him of her disappearance.

Charles fumbled unsuccessfully with the catch of his briefcase. "I assumed you knew she was taken to the County Crisis Center."

Jasmine shook her head. His words didn't ring true. "He's lying."

Charles clutched the still unfastened briefcase and bolted toward the door. "I refuse to stand here and listen to insults."

Rand moved in front of the exit, physically blocking his departure. Charles skidded to a halt, his open briefcase dangling from his hand.

Jasmine glanced down and saw an airline ticket folder and banded hundred-dollar bills inside the briefcase. Did Charles know they were on to him? Had they interrupted his getaway?

Rage pounded through her heart, surged through her veins. After all he'd done to her mother and father, he wasn't getting away. "You committed my mother so Irene could marry Talbot, didn't you. You paid off the hospital administrator, kept my mother drugged. For years your plan worked—until Talbot wanted a divorce. Then you decided to kill your best friend."

"You really are delusional." Charles's attempt at a shrug came off more as a flinch. "I suppose just like all the other times, you can't back up your accusations?"

"Ah, this time I do have proof." Jasmine raised her brows triumphantly. "You were careful, I'll give you that. But how do you think I found Lily?"

For the first time, uncertainty clouded Charles eyes. "Belle's always hated me. She's lied to you."

"Belle never said a word." Jasmine realized Charles must have threatened the poor woman into silence. "While we were in the attic, we found part of an old invoice from Bayside Hospital, with Lily's name written on it."

"So?"

Jasmine whipped out his travel papers and pointed to his scribbling on the envelope. "It's your handwriting on that slip of paper," Jasmine bluffed. "You've been paying Lily's bills for years."

Charles sneered. "My handwriting proves nothing except I paid Lily's bills to a very expensive private hospital. She needed care. She was crazy. Just like you."

"Says who?" A stranger wearing a familiar-looking baseball cap slipped from behind Rand and into the room. Annoyed at the interruption, baffled by her raging suspicions, Jasmine realized she'd seen the man before.

Charles's eyes widened in horror. Blood drained from his face, leaving him with a sickly pallor.

Jasmine eyed the man curiously. He faced her and took his hat off with a sweeping bow. "Let me introduce myself. I'm your father, Talbot Moore."

Chapter Fourteen

Talbot Moore? Her father?

"You're supposed to be dead!" Charles shouted.

On legs that had suddenly turned to jelly, Jasmine faced Talbot Moore. No wonder the man seemed familiar; she'd seen his picture hanging in Moore House. But more than a memory of a picture caused her to recognize him. He'd been the man at Bayside Hospital who had trailed after her the day she'd first found her mother. And she'd seen him follow her into the County Crisis Center.

Oh, God! She slumped into a chair and dropped her face into her hands. Had her father and Charles worked together, first to get rid of Lily and then Jasmine? She couldn't bear to think that not only didn't her father want her, he'd tried to kill her. What kind of family had she found?

"So did Irene help you try to murder me?" Talbot asked Charles, interrupting Jasmine's thoughts. Her father's question implied he'd had nothing to do with Charles's plan. Jasmine's heart lifted, and she realized she had been too quick to judge the man and his motives.

"Irene's innocent," Charles shouted. "She knew nothing about starting a fire—"

"Bingo." Talbot raised his brows in satisfaction. "That's as good as a confession for me."

Charles's face turned crimson with fury. "I didn't mean…I didn't say…"

Rand moved from in front of the door to Jasmine's side and placed a supportive hand on her shoulder. "It's all right. We've got him."

She caught Rand watching her with a wry grin. But his eyes were haunted with a concern she didn't understand.

Talbot turned to Jasmine. "I didn't know I had a daughter until you showed up at Moore House." He paused awkwardly. "If I had known, I would have been a part of your life."

Her throat tightened. Talbot hadn't known he had a daughter. He hadn't rejected her. That meant Lily had never told him about her. Slowly Jasmine realized her father was on her side. While she had no idea why he'd followed her to Bayside Hospital, she finally understood he meant her no harm. "I've always wanted a father. But I don't understand why Lily…"

"Didn't tell him?" Charles sneered. "Because I convinced her to leave him."

"What?" Her father looked so sad, her heart went out to him. Apparently, even after all these years, he still felt something for Lily.

Charles snorted. "It wasn't hard to convince Lily that staying with Talbot would hurt his career. After all, Talbot was destined to build an empire. I told her she was a nobody who would only hold him back."

Rand walked to Talbot and put a steadying hand on his shoulder as her father blinked away a tear.

"She never told me. I thought she didn't want me. Lily was the love of my life. I didn't care about her background. I told her that three years later when she came to the house. Why didn't she tell me about Jasmine then?"

"Oh, stop your whining," Charles said. "I made sure Lily never had a chance to tell you. Irene was the perfect wife for you. But you wanted a divorce."

Charles Wilcox was responsible for the destruction of her family. Rage and sadness for what she'd lost had her on the edge of tears. Because of him, Jasmine had grown up without parents, because of him her parents had been separated.

"You found my mother's letter and came after me?" Jasmine accused Charles.

Charles shook his head. "Blain told me about it later. The idiot has a crush on the girl who delivers the mail and wanted an excuse to talk to her, so he asked her to return Lily's letter to the sender. If *I'd* intercepted the letter, it wouldn't have been returned."

And he'd come after her, burning down her home so she wouldn't show up to ask for part of Talbot's estate. Puzzled, she turned to her father. "If you didn't know about me, why was a fourth child written into the will?"

Talbot never had a chance to answer. With Rand no longer blocking the door, Charles lunged for his freedom. As if expecting the move, Talbot grabbed him by the throat and forced Charles against the wall, cutting off his air. "I should kill you, you bastard."

Charles's eyes bulged. Rand seemed content to let Talbot do whatever he wanted, and Jasmine had no inclination to stop her father, either. The thirst for revenge almost overpowered her. She couldn't imagine how he must feel—betrayed by his best friend, the love of his life sent to a mental hospital, awareness of his daughter's existence denied him.

Charles deserved Talbot's punishment. But she didn't want him dead. She wanted to get to know her father, and she couldn't if he was behind bars for Charles's murder.

Charles's face turned red, his feet kicked feebly.

"Let him live so the law can deal with him," Jasmine suggested.

Talbot acted as if he hadn't heard her. Tenaciously, Charles hung on to the briefcase. Suddenly, he slipped a hand inside, retrieved a gun and aimed the weapon directly at Jasmine.

"Let me go," he wheezed to her father, "or I kill her."

Reluctantly Talbot took one step backward. Charles gasped for air, the gun wavered. In an instant, Talbot again closed in on Charles. Rand leapt across the room to help. Charles fired. The acrid scent of gunpowder filled Jasmine with fear. With three men fighting in such close quarters, either Rand or her father could have been shot.

His face a mask of pain, Talbot staggered to one side, and blood spurted from his upper arm. Her father had stepped between her and the gun, risking his life to save hers.

Talbot toppled to the floor, leaving Rand to disarm Charles. The two men fought for control of the weapon, before Rand slammed Charles's gun hand into the wall.

Charles grunted, and the gun dropped and skidded across the floor, stopping at Jasmine's feet.

Hesitantly, she picked it up. She'd never fired a weapon. In the crowded office, she could just as easily shoot Rand by accident as Charles. Fright had every bone in her body chilled and shaking.

Charles threw a wild punch at Rand's jaw. Rand ducked beneath Charles's arm, grabbed his elbow and shoved it behind the older man's back before flinging him to the floor. Charles's grunt of pain didn't deter Rand. He followed through by holding down the older man, his knee in Charles's back.

Dylan burst through the door.

"About time you got here," Rand muttered.

Dylan bent and handcuffed Charles. "I was checking with Sinclair and Moore's supply foreman. He told me Charles has a penchant for borrowing propane tanks and not returning them. The dates he took the tanks coincide with the fires."

"That proves nothing. I...I have a grill at Moore House. I barbecue—" Charles sputtered.

"Tell it to the judge," Rand muttered.

At least Rand was all right. He didn't appear to have a scratch, and relief ran through her as she released the breath she'd been holding.

Although she'd done no more than pick up the gun, Jasmine felt as battered and bruised as if she'd gone a round with a heavyweight champion. The tension in her neck had her wincing. She ached behind her eyes, and her gut churned from charging adrenaline. With a trembling hand, she laid the gun on the desk.

Dylan used his radio and called the dispatcher. "Mr. Moore needs an ambulance."

"You can't do this," Charles protested. "You've got no evidence."

Amazing! Charles had just shot Talbot, threatened

her with the same weapon and still claimed they had no evidence. Talk about delusional. But she wouldn't waste another thought on him. She had a father to aid.

A father. After thinking him dead for so long, believing he was a flesh-and-blood man and not a ghost didn't come easy. Jasmine numbly realized she had found both of her parents.

Office workers stopped in the hallway to gape. After assuring them everyone was all right, Rand sent them back to their offices.

Rand found a tie in Charles's desk drawer. "Everything's going to be all right," he told her gently. "You have a father who loves you. The few times I couldn't guard you, Talbot was looking after you."

In a moment Rand was gone from her side. He crossed the room and knotted the tie as a tourniquet around Talbot's arm.

Her father gestured to her and held out one arm. "Jasmine."

She jumped up and crossed the room on wobbly legs, then kneeled beside him, embracing him, careful not to jostle his wound. She prayed he would live. Aching to know him, she raised her head. "I'm glad you're alive."

"And I'm glad to meet my daughter." Her father patted her hair. "When Charles pointed that gun at you, I'd never been so frightened in my life."

Dylan yanked Charles to his feet. "I'm taking him downtown. Somehow I don't think he'll like the accommodations."

T.J., Art and Blain burst through the door and crowded the office. On his way out, Charles told the boys to take care of Irene, but Jasmine didn't move from Talbot's embrace. She'd waited too long to meet her father to give up one precious moment of his affection.

"Is it true?" Art asked, his gaze going from Rand to Talbot, his lower jaw dropping at the sight of his father.

T.J.'s frown broke into a wide grin. "Dad?"

Blain elbowed past his brothers, his hair in wild disarray, his normally laid-back tone surprisingly hostile. "Why was Charles in handcuffs? Why did you let us think you were dead?"

Jasmine edged protectively closer to Talbot. She glared at her youngest brother. "Your father...*our* father has been shot. Can't the explanations wait?"

"Wait?" Blain's fist punched the open palm of his other hand with a smack. "You want me to wait to hear why we went through a funeral and months of mourning when Dad's been alive and hasn't seen fit to tell us? I don't think so."

"It's only a flesh wound." With his free hand, Talbot smoothed back her hair. "I'll be fine."

Rand folded his arms across his chest, looking pleased. "It was pure luck Talbot survived the fire. We believed—"

"We?" Jasmine jerked, pinning Rand with her fiercest stare. It was suddenly her turn to feel anger, hurt, betrayal. Another lie. Rand had known her father was alive from the start. If she hadn't already been sitting, she would have collapsed in shock.

Recalling Rand's words in the kitchen and how he'd admitted lying to her, Jasmine finally understood. He hadn't been referring to Talbot's desire to divorce Irene. He'd been referring to the fact that her father was still alive. "Those voices I heard when I first came to the house, and later in your room, it was you and Talbot.''

Rand's eyes flickered with regret before hardening. ''I couldn't tell you.''

''I made him promise,'' Talbot added.

As if undecided where his loyalties lay, Art didn't move toward his father. In disgust, T.J. shook his head, perhaps finally realizing what protecting Irene had cost this family.

Blain, however, came forward. ''I guess I should have told you about the letter when you asked. But Charles said speaking out would hurt Mother.''

Jasmine sighed. ''I can't blame you for wanting to help your mother.''

The paramedics' arrival interrupted further discussion. Minutes later, they assured everyone Talbot would recover and rolled him away on a stretcher.

Art and Blain left, but T.J. lingered in the office. ''You and I,'' he said to Jasmine, ''got off on the wrong foot. I'd like to start over.'' He held out his hand to shake.

Sure the apology hadn't been easy for him, Jasmine ignored his hand and hugged him. ''You were trying to protect Irene.''

''That doesn't account for my conduct. I'm sorry.''

''Apology accepted,'' Jasmine replied. ''See you at the hospital.''

Jasmine's heart was full. Before coming to Moore House, she'd been alone. Now she'd found three brothers, her mother and her father. She had a family.

Rand touched her cheek, and the warmth of his palm spiraled heat through her. She stared into his smoky eyes and felt the excruciating tension that kept his emotions on a tight leash. She could only guess at what rushed beneath the surface. With a bittersweet sigh, she realized she'd fallen in love with a man who lied to her with the regularity of a Swiss watch.

AFTER HIS LIES, Rand doubted Jasmine would trust him again. He'd seen the hurt on her face. It was almost over, days of tormenting worry over her safety, and impotent frustration that he was forced to lie. Determined to tell her everything, he steeled himself for the possibility she might never want to see him again.

Driving to the hospital in his agitated state wasn't a good idea, so Rand led Jasmine into the empty lunchroom at Sinclair and Moore. She hadn't said a word since they'd left Charles's office, the silence between them mounting.

She took in the soda machine, microwave and tables and chairs with a cursory glance. "Aren't we going to the hospital to check on Talbot?"

"I wanted to talk with you alone first." Rand straddled a chair while she paced. "If not for luck, Talbot would have died in the construction site fire. He'd entered the building but stepped out a side entrance to investigate a noise. He was knocked out, thrown under a stack of insulation. After the explosion, I drove to the site, and unseen by anyone, Talbot crawled into the back seat of my car. I wanted to take him to the hospital, but he insisted he was all right."

Jasmine stopped pacing to frown at him for a moment. "Then who is buried in Talbot's grave?"

"A homeless man, seeking shelter for the night, was killed in the fire."

She shuddered at the picture he'd drawn. "Everyone just assumed the body was Talbot's?"

"Yes."

"Didn't the man have family?"

"Perhaps." Rand's doubts and pain churned anew. Had he and Talbot been too ruthless? "Talbot had seen the man before. We asked around, but never learned the man's name. The police assumed he was Talbot, and I never corrected their assumption."

Jasmine began to pace again, her expression unreadable. "Why did my father fake his death?"

Rand clenched his hands and shut his eyes, dreading the pain his admission would bring to her face. "It was my idea." He paused, raked a hand through his hair and forced his eyes open.

"Go on."

At least she was hearing him out. He should be grateful. "I've only been living at Moore House since Talbot and I concocted the plan. I have a home on the bay, where he stayed after the fire."

She hesitated but an instant. "I can understand why he wanted the arsonist to think he was dead. But what about Irene's grief? And his sons?"

"Talbot was divorcing Irene. He suspected her of the arson. And I distrusted all three of his children. For everyone to believe Talbot was dead for a few months seemed a better alternative to actually losing him forever."

A speculative light gleamed in her green eyes. "So what was the plan?"

"Talbot made out his will."

"I don't understand."

"He worded the will obliquely to cause the most problems, naming four children—everyone assumed I was the fourth since Talbot had raised me—in hopes the greedy arsonist would reveal himself. You showing up threw the needed kink in Charles's scheme. And Charles was too ingenious. Not until the twenty-five-year-old letter showed up did he begin making mistakes.''

Jasmine calmly met his gaze. ''Why couldn't you tell me about my father?''

At closer scrutiny, worry lines feathered the corners of her eyes, her brows furrowed. What had his lies done to her? For all her logical questions, there was a vulnerable air about her.

''When you first arrived at Moore House, I suspected you might have been the arsonist.''

''Me?'' The skin on her face grew tight, flushed.

''You had a motive for revenge—being deserted by your father. You even admitted you suspected Talbot of Lily's disappearance.''

The flicker of defenseless pain in her eyes contrasted with her squared shoulders. ''And later?''

''You already had so much on your mind, I was afraid you might slip. One sentence about your father in the present tense instead of the past would have given away the secret. If Talbot and I hadn't found proof of who'd tried to kill him, Talbot was going to come forward by the end of this week. I didn't think a few more days would matter.''

He saw the doubts in her eyes. But still, she gave him a wobbly smile. ''I see.''

Inhaling a shuddering breath, he forged ahead. ''Forgive me?''

She cocked her head, her smile wider, more confident. ''Promise me something?''

''If I can.'' Although he couldn't imagine denying her any request, the lawyer in him urged caution. The last thing he wanted was to disappoint her by making a promise he couldn't keep.

"Don't ever lie to me again."

Perhaps she wasn't lost to him. Perhaps she loved him. Hope rippled through him, replacing the cold hollow in the pit of his stomach with aching heat.

"I promise." He stood, opened his arms, and she flung herself against him. "I love you. I was afraid you'd never trust me again."

"Never is a very long time not to trust the man I love."

"You'll give me another chance?" he prompted.

She grinned, a hot, provocative woman's grin. "I'm going to keep a close eye on you. In fact, I'm making you my first priority."

Don't miss Dylan Wade's story in

FIRST-CLASS FATHER

by Charlotte Douglas
coming to you in July
from Silhouette Intrigue®.

Turn the page for a sneak preview…

Prologue

Jacaranda trees in full bloom arched above the street in a lavender blue haze, blocking the glare of the Florida midday sun. A gulf breeze ruffled the lacy branches and rained delicate blossoms like ticker-tape confetti onto the lawns and pavement below.

Lily Moore relaxed against the luxurious back seat of her son-in-law's car and smiled. It was a fitting homecoming.

Beside her, her husband, Talbot, reached for her hand. She could see her happiness reflected in his eyes. Their European honeymoon had ended, but their life together was just beginning. They had a twenty-five-year separation to make up for.

The car turned onto the street that led to their home, and Talbot squeezed her hand. "Close your eyes. I have a surprise."

"You're going to love it, Mother." Her daughter, Jasmine, green eyes dancing with excitement, swiveled to face her over the front passenger seat. "No peeking."

Lily closed her eyes and issued a silent prayer of thanks for being reunited with her only child. She had missed all but the first three years of Jasmine's childhood and the rest of her growing up. Now, at twenty-eight, her daughter was a beautiful young woman who would soon make Lily a grandmother.

Eyes shut tight, she felt the car slow, turn and come to a stop. Talbot released her hand, and she heard his door open, the sound of his footsteps circling the car, and the click of the door beside her.

"You can open your eyes now," he said.

She squinted in the brilliant sunlight and took his hand as she climbed from the car. Before her, the lawns of Moore House stretched back to the oaks and the three-story Victorian cottage nestled among the trees. Everything looked...different.

"Do you like it?" Talbot asked. "I had the tree service thin the oaks, and I hope you approve of the new color."

"Approve?" Emotion constricted her voice. "I love it."

Her heart swelled with affection for the man she'd loved for almost three decades. Now he had brought her home to Moore House, where he had lived for almost twenty-five years with his first wife, Irene, and he had changed the house as much as he'd changed Lily's life.

Gone was the somber brown exterior, replaced by a lovely rich cream. The oppressive oaks had been stripped of Spanish moss and pruned to allow sunlight to warm the building. Moore House, like Lily, had been liberated from its depressing past, and its future, like hers, looked bright and shining.

As if to make up for all she'd missed, providence had given Talbot and Jasmine back to her. She glanced at her husband, still robust and handsome despite his years. Fate had finally been kind to him, too.

He and Irene had been freed of the bondage of their unhappy union, and their sons T.J. and Art had proved their loyalty and competence in helping Talbot run Sinclair and Moore Construction.

The only dark spot on Lily's contentment was Talbot's youngest son, Blain, who blamed his father for his mother's unhappiness and had refused to speak to him since the divorce.

Lily shook off unpleasant thoughts. She wouldn't allow Blain's pouting to spoil her homecoming. Talbot would eventually mend that breach. As far as she was concerned, Talbot could hang the moon.

Beside her, Rand Sinclair, her son-in-law and Talbot's business partner, lowered the driver's window. "Do you want to walk to the house or ride?"

She inhaled the clear, crisp mid-April air, which smelled of freedom. "We'll walk. Meet us at the house and stay for lunch."

The car pulled away, and Lily looped her arm through Talbot's. Together they sauntered up the circular drive.

"Don't expect any changes inside," Talbot said. "I'm leaving the interior for you to redecorate to your heart's content."

He knew her so well. Nothing would please her more than turning the bleak mansion into a home, *their* home.

They climbed the broad steps, crossed the wide porch and stepped into the dark paneled foyer. Eugenia, the housekeeper Lily had hired before they left for Europe, stepped out of the kitchen at the far end of the hall. "Lunch will be ready in a half hour. Your mail is on the hall table. Several packages, too."

"More wedding presents, I'll bet." Jasmine entered from the back hall with Rand. "Why don't you open them while we wait for lunch?"

Rand gathered several packages and carried them toward the living room. Talbot followed with a large parcel under each arm.

Feeling like a child at Christmas, Lily read cards of congratulations and opened packages to find a Waterford vase, a Boehm nightingale, a sterling silver candlesnuffer and a linen tablecloth trimmed in Battenburg lace.

"This is addressed to Mother only." Jasmine picked up a box, wrapped in wrinkled brown paper and marked with an Orlando return address. "From Leslie Stratton. Who's that?"

Talbot shrugged. "She's not from your side of the family?"

Jasmine sat beside Lily and placed her arm around her. "You're looking at our side of the family. Open it, Mother, and solve the mystery."

Her curiosity fired, Lily peeled paper off the dress box-size package and lifted the lid. An envelope lay atop the tissue. She removed the letter and read aloud.

"My sister sent your wedding announcement from the Dolphin Bay paper, so I know you're no longer at the mental hospital. My mother, Janet Stratton, was a nurse there until her retirement two years ago. She died last year, but before she passed on, she gave me the package you'd left with her for safekeeping."

Lily dropped the paper as if it had burned her fingers and raised her hands to her temples where an incipient headache lurked. "I don't remember Janet Stratton or giving anyone a package."

Jasmine hugged her. "Naturally, you don't remember everything. Charles Wilcox made certain you were overmedicated all those years so you wouldn't try to escape and threaten Irene's marriage to Daddy."

Lily frowned at the painful memories. Talbot never would have married Irene if Irene's brother Charles hadn't kidnapped Lily and imprisoned her in that hospital. She pushed the unhappy thoughts away. Charles was in the state penitentiary now, and Irene, accompanied by Blain, had moved to a villa in France.

Lily stared at the package with a sudden sense of foreboding. She didn't want to look back. She wanted only to go forward. She shoved the box toward Jasmine. "Maybe you should just throw this away."

"Are you sure?" her daughter asked.

"Lily," Talbot said gently, "whatever's in there was important enough to smuggle out, away from Charles and his employees. Opening it is *your* decision, but I'll toss it, if that's what you want."

She hesitated. Maybe the package held something good from all those years of misery, something positive to look back on, instead of merely wasted years. She drew it toward her again and folded back the first layer of tissue.

"Now I know how Pandora felt," she said with a nervous laugh.

"Don't worry." In the chair across from her, Rand, his long legs stretched out before him, flashed a reassuring smile. "No matter what it is, the past is over. You have family to love and protect you now."

She nodded. No wonder Jasmine loved him. Next

to Talbot, Rand was the most considerate man she'd ever met. She picked up another envelope, addressed to Lily Ross, her maiden name, and yellowed with age. She withdrew the single sheet and began to read. Dizziness assaulted her after the first few words and she thrust the page at Jasmine.

Her brow furrowed with concern, Jasmine took the sheet and read aloud.

> "Dear Lily, forgive me for not stopping them from taking your baby—"

"What?" Talbot bolted upright in his chair, and the color drained from his face. He stared at Lily in bewilderment. "What baby?"

Lily opened her mouth to speak, but words wouldn't come. Her hands fluttered on her lap as if someone else controlled them.

"Finish the letter, Jasmine." Talbot rose, moved to the sofa on the other side of Lily and drew her close.

Jasmine, her face blank with shock, continued.

> "I would have helped you and your baby get away, but Mr. Wilcox threatened me and my family if I even breathed a word to anyone. I'm doing what you asked me to, though, about keeping your baby's belongings. I'm packing them away so you can have them back one day. I hope you find your baby. Forgive me.
>
>   Janet Stratton."

"A baby." Lily felt as if all the air had been sucked from her lungs. "How...?"

Talbot pulled her tighter. "The night you disappeared, we were together—"

"That brief time with you," she said, "was my last clear memory before Jasmine found me. But a baby? Even drugged, how could I give birth and not remember?"

"Your loss of memory isn't your fault," Jasmine reassured her, then prodded gently. "Let's see what's in the box."

With trembling fingers, Lily lifted the last layer of tissue paper. Beneath it lay two tiny white gowns embroidered with pale yellow flowers and French knots. On a card pinned to the garments was her clear but wobbly handwriting: "My baby, born February 18, 1973."

She faced Talbot, her cheeks wet with tears. "We have another child, and I don't even know if it's a boy or a girl."

Talbot took her in his arms, and she pressed her face against the broad expanse of his chest. "Don't worry, Lily, we'll find our child. I promise."

She nodded but said nothing.

Her reunion with her daughter and Talbot had taken twenty-five years. How long would it take to find her missing baby?

SILHOUETTE
INTRIGUE™

COMING NEXT MONTH

MARRIED IN HASTE Dani Sinclair

McKella Patterson had barely said 'I do' before her groom disappeared and a stranger swept her off her feet—and out of the way of a speeding truck. He told her his name was Greg Wyman—and that her marriage was a fake. But could she accept this stranger's protection?

FIRST-CLASS FATHER Charlotte Douglas

Heather Taylor had never told cop Dylan Wade that she'd had his baby. But now her son had been kidnapped, and Dylan was the only one who could help her find him... Dylan had said he still loved her—but that could change when he found out that the missing boy was his son…

NO ORDINARY MAN Suzanne Brockmann

Jess Baxter's new tenant Rob Carpenter was definitely the sexiest man she'd ever met! But no matter how hard she tried, he wouldn't let her get to know him. Then the murders started—all women who looked like her. And the profile of the killer matched Rob… Was he being set-up—or was he a murderer?

SEND ME A HERO Rita Herron

Detective Nathan Dawson had been warned about Veronica Miller's 'false alarms' but instinct told him she wasn't imagining things. Someone *was* stalking her. And he was going to risk his job—and his heart—to keep her safe. Only first they had to uncover the truth about a night she couldn't remember…

COMING NEXT MONTH FROM

Sensation

A thrilling mix of passion, adventure and drama

A MAN LIKE MORGAN KANE Beverly Barton
RANCHER'S CHOICE Kylie Brant
MAN OF THE HOUR Maura Seger
OWEN'S TOUCH Lee Magner

Special Edition

Compelling romances packed with emotion

SNOW BABY Cathy Gillen Thacker
WARRIOR'S WOMAN Laurie Paige
A MOTHER FOR JEFFREY Trisha Alexander
STRANDED ON THE RANCH Pat Warren
THE COWBOY TAKES A WIFE Lois Faye Dyer
PARTNERS IN MARRIAGE Allison Hayes

Desire

Provocative, sensual love stories

BELOVED Diana Palmer
THE BABY CONSULTANT Anne Marie Winston
THE LONE RIDER TAKES A BRIDE Leanne Banks
COWBOYS ARE FOR LOVING Marie Ferrarella
A SPARKLE IN THE COWBOY'S EYES Peggy Moreland
OVERNIGHT HEIRESS Modean Moon

9906

FREE

2 BOOKS
AND A SURPRISE GIFT!

We would like to take this opportunity to thank you for reading this Silhouette® book by offering you the chance to take TWO more specially selected titles from the Intrigue™ series absolutely FREE! We're also making this offer to introduce you to the benefits of the Reader Service™—

- ★ FREE home delivery
- ★ FREE monthly Newsletter
- ★ FREE gifts and competitions
- ★ Exclusive Reader Service discounts
- ★ Books available before they're in the shops

Accepting these FREE books and gift places you under no obligation to buy; you may cancel at any time, even after receiving your free shipment. Simply complete your details below and return the entire page to the address below. *You don't even need a stamp!*

YES! Please send me 2 free Intrigue books and a surprise gift. I understand that unless you hear from me, I will receive 4 superb new titles every month for just £2.70 each; postage and packing free. I am under no obligation to purchase any books and may cancel my subscription at any time. The free books and gift will be mine to keep in any case.

19EC

Ms/Mrs/Miss/Mr .... Initials ....

BLOCK CAPITALS PLEASE

Surname..

Address..

....

....Postcode ....

Send this whole page to:
THE READER SERVICE, FREEPOST CN81, CROYDON, CR9 3WZ
(Eire readers please send coupon to: P.O. Box 4546, DUBLIN 24.)